No .... Class ....

Author ADAMS,

Title Boss's C... KT-559-260

BRISTOL CITY COUNCIL LIBRARY SERVICE
PLEASE RETURN BOOK BY LAST DATE STAMPED

16 FEB 2006 20 NOV 2006
23 MAR 2006   15 JAN 2007
5 APR 2006
-4 MAY 2006 12 FEB 2007
-5 JUN 2006 20 FEB 2007
10 JUL 2006   28 FEB 2007

11 SEP 2006

27 SEP 2006

BR100 10 OCT 2006
20 OCT 2006

**BRISTOL OUTREACH
LIBRARY SERVICE**

BRISTOL CITY COUNCIL
LIBRARY SERVICES
WITHDRAWN AND OFFERED FOR SALE
SOLD AS SEEN

Bristol Library Service

AN 2763202 4

THE BOSS'S CONVENIENT BRIDE

THE BOSS'S CONVENIENT BRIDE

BY

JENNIE ADAMS

MILLS & BOON®

For my cherished friend Bronwyn.

First published in Great Britain 2005
Large Print edition 2005
Harlequin Mills & Boon Limited,
Eton House, 18-24 Paradise Road,
Richmond, Surrey TW9 1SR

© Jennifer Ryan 2005

ISBN 0 263 18586 9

Set in Times Roman 16½ on 18 pt.
16-0905-49487

Printed and bound in Great Britain
by Antony Rowe Ltd, Chippenham, Wiltshire

CHAPTER ONE

'I'M THIRTY-TWO years old, and tired of being fêted and pursued as one of Sydney's most eligible bachelors.' Nicholas Monroe, millionaire owner and boss of Monroe Global Security Systems, leaned back in the leather desk chair and crossed his suit-clad arms.

His gaze was sharp, direct and controlled, save for a very mild hint of irritation Claire would have missed if she hadn't come to know the enigmatic face so well in the past six months.

'I can see how that could become wearying after a while.' Claire's imagination went into overdrive, conjuring situations he might have endured. 'All those women jumping out from behind pot plants to accost you, telling you they want to have your babies—and all for the sake of your money, really. Not that I'm saying you aren't appealing in your own right.'

5

She smoothed her chainstore pleated skirt across her knees, and hoped the pulse that beat at the base of her throat wasn't visible beneath the crisp white blouse.

He was attractive, all right. Far beyond what was fair and reasonable in her opinion. All dark hair, tanned skin, and interesting angles to blend with the deep, velvety voice. He even smelled good, in a way that made her want to bury her face in him and just breathe him in for the next century or three.

The thought caused a familiar little catch in her chest, right about where her heart was located.

'There haven't been hordes of pot-plant-hiding females.' His mouth curved. 'But I've had my share of unwanted attention. And, contrary to what the media seems to believe, I really don't enjoy having my name on every Top Ten Bachelor list in existence. Frankly, it's an annoyance I could do without.'

'Especially as you move into this new, more settled phase of life that you want.'

Claire hoped she looked and sounded intelligent, understanding, enlightened. Anything other than completely oblivious as to where he was headed with this conversation and wholly besotted by him into the bargain.

Aside from all the happy-fuzzy feeling he brought out in her, she struggled just to ignore the way his shirt stretched across his muscled chest. Which probably made her as bad as all those pot-plant-hiding women.

To have muscles like that, he had to work out regularly. She pictured him sleek with perspiration, doing bench presses in some trendy city gym, and stifled a groan.

'Do you plan to announce a big change of lifestyle to the media in the hope it will get them off your back? Some actors take up an interest in monk-like religion for a while. Something like that would certainly prove a deterrent, since it would take you out of the running for a relationship.'

'That's an interesting option.' The look he gave her suggested he might think she had rocks in her head. 'I have to confess I hadn't actually thought of taking to any kind of priesthood to solve this particular set of challenges, but thanks for the thought.'

'I can't imagine you celibate, myself,' Claire blurted, then wondered if she should just bite her tongue off now and be done with it. Crushes did that to people. Made them say and do things they normally wouldn't.

Much good it did her to have this crush, anyway. He wasn't her type, and certainly wouldn't be interested in her. Millionaire bosses didn't fall for clerical pool upstarts. Not in the real world. No matter how gooey those upstarts might feel about their boss.

What had made Nicholas speak of personal things anyway, this fine January morning, ensconced in the opulent Sydney office suite overlooking the harbour? His life had been the key topic for the last five minutes. Plans, aspirations, intentions. All of them private, not business-related.

It made her uncomfortable. What had she to do with his desire to 'settle his life, move on to a new phase'?

'Are you really on every list?'

'Every one.' He gave a tight upward tilt of his firm lips. 'Apparently there are others who can't imagine me being happy alone, either.'

'I guess it's supposed to be kind of flattering, finding yourself on bachelor lists. Women who read those lists would want to...' *Spend hours making slow, languorous love with you.* She coughed. 'Get to know you better, I'm sure. If they had a chance. You know. Nice women. Ones who don't hang around behind potted palm trees.'

Claire Dalgliesh. Shut up this minute. Before you stick your foot any further down your throat.

'Perhaps you're right.' He smiled that killer smile that sent her insides crazy every time. 'I can't say I've ever given it a lot of thought.'

'Um, no.' *Good one, Claire. Comparing women to pot-plant-lurkers.* Of all the inane things she could have said. 'I don't suppose you would have.'

He leaned back in his chair in the seemingly casual pose he had used a hundred times before, but his eyes were watchful. Assessing. 'You and I have worked together closely for the past six months, since Clerical moved you up to fill in as my personal assistant.'

'I've enjoyed it.' His change of subject was off-putting. She hoped he wasn't about to tell her she was no longer needed. That would be an utter disaster. She couldn't stand the thought of not seeing him every day. Not talking with him, or laughing with him. 'It's a great job. I've valued the opportunity to get involved in the company at this level.'

'And Clerical did the right thing in recommending you for the position. You've done well.' He pulled a file from the top drawer of his desk, flipped briefly through its pages, and dropped it in front of him.

Claire recognised her personnel file, and her heart started to thump. He *was* going to dismiss her back to her old job in the pool. But why?

'In fact, you've not put a foot wrong since you started in the downstairs division three and a half years ago. Your record's impeccable.'

'Thank you.' Her brain jittered around, weighing up whether it should fly into a full-blown anxiety attack or not. So far the odds were for the attack. 'I do my best.'

He nodded, as though pleased. 'I've come to know you, Claire. You're honest, reliable, straightforward.'

At that, Claire felt a twinge of discomfort. She *had* worked hard, and had been completely transparent in every way possible. But she wondered what he would think if he knew she was keeping secrets from the law, and paying off a blackmailer into the bargain.

'I try to do my work to the best of my ability. I'm committed to Monroe's.'

'And I'm committed to the plans I have in mind for the future, Claire.' He leaned forward. 'I want you to be clear about that.'

'Clear. Yes. Certainly.' She nodded and hoped that she *looked* clear, for in point of fact she was still mystified.

'I've said that I want to change my life. The bachelor-related attention is a side issue.' He dismissed those hundreds, probably thousands of women with a flick of one elegant wrist. His steely gaze pinned hers. 'What matters to me is that I settle my future the way I want it to be settled. It's something I feel is past due. In short, my plan is marriage. To a suitable woman. Of my choosing.'

'Marriage?' The last solution Claire would have imagined he'd choose. She crossed her legs, uncrossed them again. Moved to smooth her already smoothed skirt, and stopped herself, jerking her hands back into her lap to clench around her notepad. 'I'm sure you'll find marriage very helpful if you want to become more settled.'

But what did it have to do with reviewing her work performance? Nevertheless, he wanted to get married, and that had ramifications of its own.

As the idea sank in, a jealous, possessive part of her objected violently. She didn't want him to marry. Didn't want to see some wife hanging off his arm at every turn. Fair enough that Claire herself couldn't have him. She knew that. But did he have to rub it in so thoroughly?

Suddenly, illumination struck. There could only be one reason for him to tell her all this. He must want her to help him make it happen. He wasn't going to send her back downstairs.

He'd talked up her efficiency and other qualities, so she would do her best for him with this, too.

Diabolical man. Just how much was a temporarily promoted admin assistant with a stupid crush supposed to be able to take? A lot, apparently. And she would take it, drat him, because she always did her professional best.

She lifted the notepad and poised her pencil above it. 'What sort of help can I give you? Do you have a lady in mind already? Or shall I get up a list of likely candidates? A few names come to mind, and I suppose I could scan the society columns for more.'

Would you like to see X-rays of their teeth? Hip span measurements? To hear their views on plastic surgery and liposuction for possible future reference? I can arrange all that, and more. Maybe if she remained flippant she wouldn't be tempted to cry.

'What particular attributes are you looking for?'

'No.' The solitary word cut across her questions. 'Let me explain the rest.'

He paused. In anyone else Claire might have believed it was a glint of vulnerability that flashed through the sharp hazel eyes, and as quickly disappeared. But Nicholas Monroe? Vulnerable? The idea was ludicrous. He simply wouldn't suffer from that kind of weakening attack. He wouldn't allow it.

The object of her thoughts cleared his throat. 'The thing is, I don't believe in romance. I've observed a lot of relationships, and I've seen what happens when people think they're *in love*. Their personalities alter. They go from sensible to irrational, seemingly overnight.'

'I see.' Beyond those two words she didn't know how to respond. Couldn't imagine anything that she could possibly say that would be even mildly appropriate. He was discussing love. Disparaging it, in fact. How *did* one respond when one's boss did that?

'Yes.' He laced his fingers together on top of her file. The gesture looked almost possessive, but Claire rejected this thought as soon as it formed. She was becoming fanciful. Imagine how much her boss would dislike that!

'When people believe they're in love,' Nicholas went on, 'every sane thought goes out of their heads. Simple matters become the most complicated on earth. If their partner wakes up grumpy one morning, they worry it's the end of the relationship. They tell lies because they're afraid the other person will fall out of love with them if they're too truthful.'

Claire's heart thunked into her shoes for a second, before she reminded herself this wasn't about her. She wasn't a liar, anyway. Keeping your own counsel about your problems was another thing entirely. But how could he feel like that?

'All right. I guess you obviously don't want those sorts of complications in your life.' She hoped her tone was sufficiently bland that he wouldn't guess that his attitude had shocked her.

'Correct. What I want is someone sensible, who won't be swayed by silly emotional ups and downs. Someone I'll be able to tolerate at my side for decades to come. A woman who respects, as I do, that the concept of being in love is an illusion.'

'Tolerate. Yes, right. And no being in love.' This was more like the man she knew and worked for. The vulnerability angle summarily banished, she wrote the words *'Must be able to tolerate husband who does not love her'* at the top of her notepad.

With effort, she held off from adding anything about liposuction or teeth. Then, with a confidence that was born purely of blind hope, she added, 'We'll find someone appropriate for you. Don't worry.'

Claire could do this. It wasn't as if she *really* cared about Nicholas.

'I've already found her.'

Who is she? I'll rip her throat out. Claire's pencil drew a deep, squiggly line across the page and tore through to the pages below. She forced her hand to stop, and looked up, feigning a calm expression she didn't feel. 'You have?'

'Indeed.' He seemed quite pleased about it, too. 'You understand, Claire, that I've been very impressed with your work performance?'

They were back to that again. 'I appreciate it.'

'We've tested our ability to get along with each other.' Abandoning his connection with her file, he unravelled his long, lean fingers and began to tick points off on them. 'At times we've disagreed on subjects, solutions to problems, ways to move on a matter.'

The first time that had happened Claire had worried for a whole day that she might have blown her job. She conjured up what she hoped was an agreeable sort of smile. 'We have. But we've always managed to work things out.'

'Exactly.' He carried on with his points. 'Sometimes I've been short with you. At other times you've been frustrated with me. We've weathered the crises, the deadlines, the days when everything went sour. We've coped well because we're both straightforward people, and particularly because neither of us has brought our emotions into the working relationship. I admire that about you, Claire.'

'You do?' She tried to clear the croak out of her throat. 'Um, that is, you do?'

He nodded. 'You keep a cool head. You look at things in a sensible manner. Business partnerships thrive on sensible, unemotional standards, and so will the kind of marriage I have in mind.'

'I'm...glad...you feel that way.' *I'm stunned you feel that way. That you have such a cynical view of love. That you believe people devalue themselves somehow if they allow their emotions to come into play.* 'I'm sure you'll be very comfortable in the kind of relationship you have in mind.' *With whatever poor woman you believe will fit your criteria.* Claire was beginning to believe that she, herself, really would be better off out of it.

'Then perhaps it's time I told you exactly who I have in mind for this relationship.'

She unconsciously straightened. 'Please do.'

'You, Claire,' he said, 'happen to be the only woman I can imagine filling the role of my wife.'

The words did pass through her eardrums. It was just that her brain would only absorb them to a certain degree. All she knew was he wanted to get married and he already had the woman picked out. He hadn't needed to mention any of this to her, and make her heart break out in chilblains, let alone make her think she would have to measure hip spans.

A spark of anger flared. So what? She didn't even care. 'I'm sure that would be exactly— *What?*'

Did she have wax in her ears? Claire could think of no other explanation for mishearing him so completely.

'Pardon me, but I thought you just said that I—'

'I said it.' He lowered his head and proceeded to stare her down through the lock of thick black hair that had flopped over onto his high, intelligent forehead. Waiting. Expectantly. For her to say something.

She did. And she hardly had to work at all to keep her hand from reaching for that errant lock and smoothing it in one long, sensual, inviting sweep. The man had asked her to marry him.

How wonderful! To marry the boss, the man of her dreams. Her stomach did a backflip. Panic stirred to life somewhere at the centre of her psyche and threatened to shut down all systems permanently. She couldn't comprehend this.

'Right. I see. You think I would be the best choice for the position of Mrs Nicholas Anthony Monroe, now that you've decided there should be one? A Mrs Monroe, I mean.'

Even as she spoke she expected him to laugh and tell her this was all some sort of joke or something. He had to laugh, right? But he didn't. Her boss really had just asked her to marry him.

Her lungs did their best to fold in on themselves, but Claire forced herself to breathe deeply and slowly through her nose. She could deal with this. It was a piece of cake.

No, I can't deal with this. It's mad. Insane. Totally off the planet. And he has to know it.

She scrambled to pull her stunned thoughts together. There had to be some way to understand this. To get it to make sense. He wanted to marry her. Out of the blue. Without any warning whatsoever. It was fantastic. Unbelievable. Terrifying.

It was a completely unemotional invitation. Claire's joyous bubble popped. He might as well have asked her to pull a report, or update the virus software on their inter-office computer network. *'Why?'*

'Why you, Claire?'

Yes. Out of all the women he could have asked, why ask her? She nodded mutely.

'I've come to know you, and I've realised what a trophy you would be. I want you at my side.'

'I see. A prize. *Sans* emotions, of course.' She tried to make it sound as though she were amused.

It was true that she had a brain like an electronic organiser, but that was a small, insignificant part of her overall make-up. She was also caring, emotional, *feeling*. What a way for him to describe her. She might as well go out and throw herself off the edge of a cliff right now.

But he wasn't finished with her yet. 'You're also naturally charming, and capable enough to cope with any hostess duties that might come your way.'

'Thank you.' She took care to keep the sarcasm from her tone, but there was something innately insulting in such a cold assessment of her character. In this man thinking she would appreciate being seen as nothing more than an animated wife-doll who would stand at his side and make all the right noises.

'You'd have anything you wished, of course—within reason.' He waved a hand. 'As my wife, you would enjoy a wealthy lifestyle.'

All those millions, offered so casually. Had he any idea what he was throwing out there? She wasn't avaricious, but he couldn't know that. Couldn't know just how driven she was in the money department at the moment.

Nothing was worth sacrificing her ideals about love and marriage, though. Not even a convenient way to end her cash problems a little more quickly. Not that she would ever take advantage of marrying him to get money. Besides, her efforts to take care of the situation were going okay. She was getting there. Slowly.

Nicholas was, ironically, the key to her plan, but as her high-paying *boss*, not as a potential life mate conveniently loaded with the green stuff. Claire was well shot of him, too, if this was the best he could offer.

'I don't know what to say.' Or perhaps she just didn't know *how* to say it. Or whether there would be consequences *to* saying it. She had seen him crush business opponents who got on the wrong side of him. Just how would he react to her turning him down? It was the smart choice. Despite everything, her heart protested at this. But she quelled the reaction.

'Don't you, Claire? I believe you'll say yes.' His gaze held hers briefly before it dropped away. One long finger drummed on the desktop, then stopped abruptly. 'It's a valid offer. One I think you'll understand and appreciate.'

'You think I'll agree?'

A part of her *was* tempted. The part that was still stupidly attracted to him, against all odds. But one irrefutable fact remained. A fact that happened to be important to her. Nicholas didn't love her. His feelings came nowhere near that. From his attitude right now, she imagined they never would.

Her chin lifted in determined defiance. She didn't love him, either. Oh, maybe a little...

But, *no*. She really, really didn't love him. At all. He attracted her, yes, but it wasn't the same thing. Those other little twinges hadn't meant anything. Really. At least she had been smart enough not to fall for him completely.

She put her notepad and pencil down on the edge of the desk as her heart began to beat hard again. 'Theoretically, if I didn't take you up on this offer, what would happen?'

'Examining all the angles, Claire? You never can contain that thoroughness, can you?' Again his gaze sloughed over her and slid away, and again his face closed into an arrogant, confident mask.

'Not really, no. It's too ingrained in my nature.'

She had always been the thinker, the one to worry about consequences, while Sophie took life by the throat and couldn't care less.

The chalk and cheese sisters, their parents used to call them, and it was apt. Sophie still played at life without a safety net. And Claire still worried about, and dealt with, consequences.

Hence Sophie's stupid action of 'borrowing' money from her boss to fund the high-flying lifestyle she thought would impress the man she wanted to marry.

Sophie had lost track of the extent of her *borrowing*. She had snared Senator Tom Cranshaw in the end, but a month before the wedding was due to take place the man she was working for had discovered what she had done and decided it would be a good opportunity to blackmail her.

Either she met his demands to pay instalments of money that added up to far more than what she'd stolen, or he would reveal her actions to both the police and the press. Sophie would go to jail for embezzlement, and, because he was about to marry her, the Senator's career would take a hit from which he would probably never recover.

Sophie had run crying to her sister, of course. Confessing all and begging for help. That had been over a year ago, and Claire was still working her way through the mess, with one final payment to take care of three months from now.

She didn't like that Sophie had hidden the truth from Tom—any more than she liked that her sister had dumped almost all of the financial responsibility for this onto Claire. But it was too late now. They were in too deep. There was no going back.

'If you declined my marriage offer, you'd go back to the clerical pool earlier than planned.' Nicholas's words brought her train of thought to an abrupt halt. 'After today's discussion, I would prefer to go onward working with someone less *aware*, shall we say, of my personal aspirations.'

He delivered this verdict on her fate without a blink, even though he had just issued her with a devastating and thoroughly untenable ultimatum. His shoulders tensed beneath the suit. 'Not that I expect a negative outcome.'

What was she supposed to do now?

You'll be able to fix it, Claire. You always know what to do. Sophie's words rose to haunt her.

I love my sister, and I will protect her, and one day she'll realise how much I care about her and love me back. She loves me even now.

She just isn't very good at showing it, that's all.

Claire would figure a way out of this—because Nicholas couldn't send her back to the clerical pool yet, and that was all there was to it. 'Why demote me if I say no? It would result in a massive pay-cut for me. That doesn't seem fair.'

Now that she had her feelings under a bit more control, it frustrated her that she was trying to be noble, not to have a mercenary bone in her body. And here was Nicholas, threatening to take her nice fat paycheque away from her unless she married him.

As administrative assistant to the boss she received five times her normal salary, and she needed every cent.

'Janice isn't due to return for ages yet.'

'I'm aware of that.' His reserved tone matched the cool green flecks in his eyes. The jut of his jaw sent warning signals blasting over her. 'Just as you're aware that this position has never been guaranteed. You could have found yourself back in the clerical pool at any time, for any number of reasons. Or for no reason, if I happened to decide I wanted to make a change.' He sat forward in his chair with a jerk. 'Let's get to the point. What's your answer?'

Did she have a choice? It would be madness to accept him. Yet how could she say no? She *had* to have that extra money.

'What you've outlined,' she ventured, knowing it was a last-ditch effort to stave off the inevitable but unable to stop herself anyway, 'doesn't sound a very cosy sort of relationship.'

Heat sparked into his eyes for just a moment, in a wave of scalding intensity. 'Oh, I think you'd find we'd be perfectly *cosy.*'

The sheer sensual power of his statement stole her breath. She reacted to him with a responding wave of sexual heat. She might have disabled her emotions, but her hormones were a little more difficult to subdue, apparently.

'I never realised you—' She broke off, and this time her sense of panic was even greater.

Things were spiralling out of control. She felt as though she had accidentally climbed onto a rollercoaster on top of a high building—

wind blasting her, everything whirling around, nothing firm beneath her searching feet.

'You weren't meant to realise.' He laid his hands on the mahogany desk. Large, well-formed hands, that had never touched her beyond the brushing of fingers to give or receive a file, or to pass a telephone.

Hands that, if she married him, would travel her body in all the ways she had imagined and more. But in lust, just lust, she reminded herself.

'Until I made the decision to marry you,' he said, 'it would have been a mistake to let you see that.'

'I understand. I guess that's—ah—a level-headed outlook to take at this point.' She barely knew what she was saying, but *she* would need to be level-headed if she hoped to find a way through this situation that wouldn't end in disaster.

That meant she had to overcome her panic. To get her heart to stop thundering and her senses to untangle from the swirling uproar they'd got themselves into. 'You've taken me by surprise with all of this.'

Unable to endure looking into that magnetising face a moment longer, she rose from the chair and moved to the bank of floor-to-ceiling glass that overlooked the bay. The seas of Sydney Harbour outside appeared calm, virtually unruffled.

In contrast, Claire was a churning cauldron of panic and stress and disillusionment. 'Do you really never want love? A melding of hearts as well as minds?' She kept her back turned, addressing the words to his shadowy reflection in the glass. Surely some small part of him longed for those things? 'Don't you believe that can happen sometimes? To some people at least?'

'No. Love—the kind you're referring to—is nothing more than an illusion.'

His words were clipped and she continued to stare through the glass of the high-rise suite, oblivious now to the harbour activity below.

'People want to believe in some fairytale ideal, to believe that some transitory feeling can actually keep their marriages together.' His tone harshened. 'In truth, marriages survive or not, depending on the level of determination of the partners to make a go of it—and on their suitability in the first place.'

'How sad.' She spoke the words beneath her breath, and then turned to face him. To search for the reason he held such an unrelenting, rejecting view on the subject. 'Your parents are divorced, aren't they? Is that why—?'

'Don't think I had a disastrous childhood, Claire. I didn't.' He inclined his head, all sign of emotion carefully locked away once more behind the corporate mask. 'Yes, my parents are proof that what I say is true, but I would have formed that conclusion anyway. Given the divorce statistics, it's the only logical thing to believe.'

'And logic is everything?' Had he wrapped himself so deeply in reasoning that he could no longer see the emotional side of life? She didn't want to believe it. There had to be a live, feeling man in there somewhere.

Just waiting to be rescued with the warmth of a woman's love? With the warmth of her love? She would have to be crazy even to try it. Doubly crazy to try it in her current circumstances.

'That's right.' Unaware of her thoughts, he gave her an approving glance. 'Compatibility is what counts. If two people can work together for the same goals, that makes them a really strong team. We'll have that, Claire, and we'll be happy. I'm certain of it.'

'Happy.' But love *could* happen. He was wrong about that. Not that it made any difference to her now. She searched the aristocratic face, with its winged brows and firm, straight nose, and forced herself to accept the dictates of fate—and her situation.

They would never reach marriage, she would make certain of that, but she would have to agree to the idea for now. She drew a deep breath and willed her voice not to quiver.

'I accept your proposal.'

CHAPTER TWO

THE grooves beside Nicholas's mouth deepened, curved into something more than sternness but less than a smile. 'Thank you, Claire. You've made me a happy man.'

A certain stiffness eased out of his posture. He had probably been poised to banish her back to the clerical pool post-haste if she said no to his preposterous marriage proposal!

'You might end up sorry you ever asked.'

In fact, I'm quite sure of it. Although I doubt you'll be half as sorry as I am right at this moment.

She glanced at the calendar on the wall. Today was Thursday. On a Thursday three months ahead exactly, Sophie would finally be out of the clutches of her ex-boss. The day and date for that final payment were stamped indelibly on Claire's consciousness.

She recalled another significant Thursday from a history lesson long since gone. The

33

Wall Street Crash of 1929 had occurred on a Thursday, and it had eventually led to the Great Depression.

At this point the comparison seemed apt.

Well, the words had been spoken now. They couldn't be taken back. But she could and would take control of what happened next. Of everything that happened from here on. She had to if she didn't want to go mad.

'As I said, I accept your proposal, but I do have conditions.'

'Do you?' One brow rose in haughty enquiry. 'Spit them out. I'm all ears.'

All ears and aggressive waiting. She couldn't let him intimidate her.

'What I would like to suggest is a six-month engagement period.' Her glance was direct, determined. Calm, she hoped. 'We may have worked together for a while, but I couldn't go ahead with such a major step as marriage without getting to know you a whole lot better than I do now.'

In a written contract she would have referred to this as the escape clause. The six-month period would allow plenty of time for her to make the final payment to Sophie's black-mailer, break off the engagement, and walk away. Nicholas would have to accept it. Would have to accept that she had left room for doubt right from the start.

I'm sorry, Nicholas, but on reflection I've decided I can't marry you after all. We just wouldn't suit, you see, because I'm a romantic and you're—well, you're not.

There would be no position for her then, even in the clerical pool. Indeed, it would be unbearable to stay on. She would leave Monroe's, and Nicholas, for ever. It was a price she would have to pay.

'Unless you had planned to wait longer than that to marry, anyway?'

'No.' The uncompromising word suited the man who had uttered it. 'I see no point in prevaricating once my mind is made up. In fact, I'd prefer to make the period of engagement three months.'

He stood from his chair, the sleek lines of his body hard beneath the tailored grey suit.

In moments he was at her side. His broad shoulders loomed over her lighter frame, crowding her, making her aware of him all over again. Of his strength, his scent, and the aura of power that surged through every square inch of him, calling to every part of her.

'That's more than enough time for you to get to know me in any way you feel is lacking at this stage. I see no need for us to wait longer.'

Claire fought the pull of attraction that urged her to forget reason, to break out of her caution and give him whatever he wanted. With interest.

'Five months would be better.'

She gave him the benefit of a determined look down the length of her nose. Not an easy feat when she had to look up at him to do it. When she wanted to melt into a puddle at his feet and agree to anything he suggested, and then some.

His irritation showed in the deepening furrow between the sharp, piercing eyes. 'Four months.'

Claire ran mental calculations. If everything went okay she should be able to manage it. Provided they didn't go into extravagant plans that could get too complicated too soon. 'All right. I'm willing to accept that. Four months it is.'

All she needed now was a little time to pull herself together. To get control of the maddening awareness that arced and jolted through her, that insisted she get closer, despite how stupid that would be. To stop her foolish emotions from trying to do cartwheels of excitement because Nicholas had asked her to marry him. She could rest assured that *his* emotions hadn't been anywhere near the building at the time.

He smiled. The cat that had got the cream. 'We'll marry on the first Saturday after those four months are up. So you're even gaining a couple of days on top of your bargain. You should be pleased. You negotiate well.'

'When I'm falling in with your terms.' It felt more like a sentence than an agreement. She couldn't share his pleasure.

'Something like that,' he agreed.

From here, she could reach out and touch his jaw if she wanted. Could trace the tanned skin that even this early in the day carried a hint of dark beard stubble. Could ruffle his thick black hair. The knowledge that she *did* want to do all of those things didn't help her state of mind.

'What of your other conditions?' For a moment heat had darkened his eyes again, but it was masked now. He glanced at the view, then turned back to her. 'You'll be well provided for should I drop dead early, if that's the kind of thing you're wondering about.'

'It's not.' She drew a steadying breath. This was the tricky part. 'I'd like to keep our engagement secret, then marry quietly when the four months is up.'

'Why?' The warmth melted away as though it had never been.

Because that way there'll be no fuss when I call it all off.

'I don't like fanfare, and my sister…' In this instance Sophie would prove conveniently useful. 'Sophie's out of the country. She and Tom are taking an extended vacation in Europe. After that they plan to visit some of our neighbouring countries, to drum up good feeling for Australia.'

'Along with good feeling for Senator Tom Cranshaw.' Nicholas knew of her brother-in-law's political aspirations. His bland comment was a statement of fact, nothing more. 'What do they have to do with keeping things secret until our marriage?'

'My sister is all I have in the way of family. I want to tell her about this face to face.' *I'll never breathe a word of it to her at all, and I'm sorry for letting you believe otherwise, but I have no choice.* 'It would upset me if she read it in the newspapers, or heard it some other impersonal way.'

'Why not simply phone her?' His stark tone left no room for argument. 'Give her the news, and we can get on with our plans without worrying about secrecy.'

'Not good enough.' She injected an equal measure of determination into her answer. 'It has to be face to face. That's it.'

After what seemed interminable minutes, but was probably only seconds, he spoke. 'How long will she be gone?'

'As of today?' The section of Claire's brain labelled *Calendar* materialised on the insides of her eyelids. 'Three and a half months.' Two weeks after the final blackmail payment had to be made. Given Claire's predicament, the time-frame was convenient. 'I want my sister at my wedding. I don't want to marry until after she gets back, and I'm determined to tell her my news in person.'

'All right. We keep things quiet. But the moment your sister returns to Australia you tell her, and we go ahead with our small, discreet wedding on the date we've agreed.' He didn't seem particularly pleased, but nor did he seem aggravated beyond measure. 'In the end it makes little difference how we go about it, I suppose, as long as the marriage goes ahead.'

'Good. Thank you.' Claire let out a single, shuddering breath. She was a long way from being out of the woods, but she could handle this. Once her nerves stopped jumping and the panic subsided and she could use her lungs properly again....

It was doable. *Wasn't it?*

'We'll sign the Notice of Intended Marriage and other necessary papers today.' Nicholas gestured for Claire to return to the desk.

Maybe if she were seated again he would be able to ignore the way the navy skirt and soft cream blouse clung lovingly to every curve and indent of her shapely figure. Then again— his gaze skimmed over her once more—maybe not.

The sooner he had this matter signed and sealed, the better. He didn't like loose ends, and wanting Claire Dalgliesh had definitely turned into a loose end since he had decided he would like her as his marriage partner. At times it was all he could do to banish thoughts of her from his mind.

'You really were sure of me, weren't you?' Her husky voice slid through his senses, causing a tightening in his gut, a tautening of muscles as his body reacted to that unconscious sexiness.

From the top of her deep gold hair to the toes of her slender, tanned feet she exuded her own brand of sensual appeal—the more effective because it appeared to be completely unconscious. Her brown eyes held untapped secrets that called a challenge to him.

He wanted to see her in the heat of passion, to see what those rich orbs would reflect then. Desire? Lust? The thought of her nails raking his back, of her moaning his name slid through his mind, and he drew a sharp, controlling breath.

'Sure of you?' *Maybe.* 'What I'm sure of, Claire, is that this is right.'

Something deep down told him that. He convinced himself it was the same instinct that had made him a success and kept him that way in business.

Claire slid into the seat across the desk from him, crossed her long legs, and reached for the documents. Her hands were shaking, he noted. 'Don't we need a marriage celebrant or a justice of the peace present for something like this?'

'We do.' He pressed a button on his phone system. 'Would you send the Reverend up, please?'

'You already had him here? How long...' She cleared her throat as she flicked through the prepared sheets. 'How long does it take to give notice that you plan to marry?'

'A month and a day.' He had investigated this marriage idea from all angles before he approached her. Could tell her anything she wanted to know about it. He couldn't explain his sense of eager expectation, though, other than to put it down to the kind of feeling he got when he was approaching the closure of a particularly important deal. 'If I had to I could get it back to a week, or even a day.'

Claire looked first shocked, then nervous. 'Oh.'

Nicholas spotted movement beyond the door, and rose swiftly to usher the middle-aged cleric into the room. 'Thank you for waiting, Reverend. We're set to go ahead now.'

He introduced the man, then indicated the top form in front of Claire. 'Can you type your details straight in, Claire? We'll take care of the rest in a moment.'

'Yes, of course.'

It was a short time only before she returned to them.

Once the details were covered, and a time agreed for the ceremony, the Reverend stood to take his leave. Nicholas wasn't interested in bandying pleasantries now that their business was over, and the man seemed to sense that.

'If you have any questions, or would like to discuss anything further,' the Reverend said, 'I'm more than willing to make myself available. Otherwise, please contact me when you're ready to talk about the style of marriage service, and so on.'

After the Reverend had left, Claire turned to Nicholas. Her smile seemed forced. 'What church is he from? I would have thought most places would be booked up at least a year in advance.'

He named the denomination, and shrugged. 'I give financial support to the charitable arm of that particular organisation. I didn't ask about their booking schedule, but obviously our request wasn't a problem for him. I've booked the church, however, if you don't want to marry there, we can move it to a court house.'

The thought of marrying her in that clinical environment bothered him. He shook the feeling off. Of course it made no difference.

'Oh, no. The church is fine. I have…no objection to traditional weddings.' She glanced at her desk. 'Was there anything else before I get back to work?'

'Lunch with the Forresters at one p.m. And buzz through to John Greaves and tell him I want his progress report on the Campbell job right away.' A sense of relief crept through him. 'Choose a nice place for lunch with the Forresters,' he added. 'Then phone the wife to line it up. They'll be *en route* somewhere up the coast at this moment, in their yacht, but you have her cellphone number on file. If they're running late, we'll do dinner tonight instead.'

'I'll get right on it.' She turned to leave, giving him a glorious view of the stretch of her skirt across the trim expanse of her buttocks as she moved.

'Oh, and Claire?'

'Yes?'

'I'll want you with me. So organise a temp from downstairs to cover in your absence, and to help with any catching up later.'

He smiled—pleased with her, pleased with his plans. Pleased that from now on Claire would be spending a great deal more of her time in his company. It would be...fun. He frowned a little, then gave himself a mental shake.

'In fact, put someone on standby to help out whenever we want for the rest of the week. I may decide to take you out with me at other times as well.'

She inclined her head. 'As you wish.'

He paced towards her. For a moment, awareness and anticipation were revealed clearly on her face. She expected him to kiss her, and her gaze softened, igniting a responding something in him.

Nicholas pushed the reaction down. Did she want him to seal their marriage agreement in the traditional way? In the way romantics dreamed of? He wouldn't do that. He would kiss Claire when *he* chose, for his own reasons. But he knew it would be soon. Very soon. He stopped abruptly, several steps away.

'Don't you want to ask me about the future of your position with the firm? You seemed very interested in it earlier.'

Her gaze flew to his and locked there. 'I don't want to give up this job.' For a moment she looked panicked, but then she stuck her chin out in clear challenge. 'Despite my eminent replaceability, which you've made more than clear, I happen to like my role as your assistant. I even believe I do it rather well.'

She *was* good at her job. She'd been very efficient, these past months, while Janice recovered from her car accident that had almost killed her. Had he threatened Claire with a return to the clerical pool simply to make her agree to marry him? He didn't want to think he could be that calculating, but was there a tiny possibility?

No. Only desperate people behaved that way, and Nicholas Monroe didn't get desperate. He hadn't done so when his middle-aged assistant had almost up and died on him, and he certainly wasn't desperate about Claire, either. She suited his purposes, that was all. He thrust the thoughts from him.

'Then you stay on.' At least until they married. For one thing, he wanted her where he could see her, touch her, whenever and however he pleased. She would have to get used to that, to accepting his acts of possession. 'I think that will work very well.'

'I...uh...' She cleared her throat. 'Okay.'

He let his gaze wander blatantly over her, his desire a blaze that heated his skin, that made him prickle and itch beneath the conservative constraints of the suit. *Sex and companionship.* That was what they would share.

It would be a good marriage. A smart one. Between two well-suited people. 'We've discussed this enough for now. Let me know if there are any problems arranging our lunch with the Forresters.'

'I will.' She gave a cool nod and tucked a stray wisp of hair behind her left ear, but a pulse beat sharp and strong at the base of her throat.

She wanted him as much as he wanted her, and the thought pleased him. Immensely. *This* was what it was all about. 'Thank you, Claire. That's all for now.'

'Okay.' A cautious smile touched her full lips. Her mouth was unconventionally wide, her nose slightly too strong to meet the stereotype of typical femininity. He rather liked both aspects. He also liked it when she smiled for him.

Smile, pant, gasp. He wanted it all—and why not? She would soon be his wife.

Nicholas allowed himself a second satisfied smile, careful to turn his back first, so she didn't see it. Then he turned his mind back to business. Because Monroe's was, after all, about business.

Marriage proposals aside, work was what made Nicholas Monroe tick.

CHAPTER THREE

AFTER her boss's shock proposal, Claire had wanted time to think, but she didn't get it. Theirs was a busy office, and it felt like only minutes before they were on their way to meet Nicholas's clients. They were discussing the Forresters now.

'Jack is dangling a carrot for us, that's all.' Nicholas manoeuvred his silver Porsche effortlessly through the traffic. 'If we win him over, Monroe's gets the chance to install and maintain security systems in more than a dozen marinas up and down the New South Wales and Queensland coasts. He owns a hell of a lot more property than that, too. Hotels, motels, restaurants. You name it. He also holds a lot of sway in the business community. A recommendation from him would go a long way. If we got security on all his properties, we'd be talking serious money at that point.'

50

'He'll sign up with us.' Claire watched the other vehicles move by, the traffic lights ahead change from red to green. She was trying hard to keep her racing thoughts under control, to stop herself from sliding back into the emotional basket weaving that had been going on since he proposed.

In out, in out, round and round and round, in an unending whirl. It wasn't easy to control it, but she couldn't let him see how truly rattled she was. Later, when she was alone, she could indulge in a nice, private meltdown.

'We've got the best security systems in Australia,' she said now. 'Possibly in the whole Southern Hemisphere. Once he's tried them, he'll see that, and move all his property over to us.'

The city teemed, as usual. And this discussion with Nicholas was predictable, too. It showed him at his most businesslike and unemotional. The familiarity should have helped her to relax, but she was beyond that at the moment.

For Nicholas might have been mouthing business matters, but any time he looked at her his eyes were full of a powerful sensual heat that left her panting. When she had given the necessary agreement to his marriage proposal, she hadn't considered how much he might physically want her, or that he would be totally unafraid to show it. Nor how deeply that open wanting would affect her.

Her senses responded. That was bad.

Her emotions responded. *That* was far worse. Hope kept trying to well up in her heart, and she kept having to squash it down again.

His emotions weren't involved. She needed to remember that.

Endeavouring to ignore her reaction to the fire in his eyes, she forced herself to focus on the discussion. 'If Mr Forrester is smart enough to build a business empire, surely he's smart enough to appreciate the kind of technology Monroe's has on offer.'

'I appreciate your confidence in our ability, both to produce and to impress.' His voice held a slight smile. 'Ah.' He slotted the car into a parking space. 'Only a short walk away.'

'Does everything always fall into place for you?' She covered the wistful question with a flippant smile, not wanting him to guess how she envied the apparent smoothness of his life, while hers had been in a mess even *before* this day started. It was far worse now, and, like Wall Street's Black Thursday, was only going to go downhill from this point.

Pessimistic, aren't you?

Huh. Actually, she wasn't being pessimistic. For once she was doing just as Nicholas would like, and assessing the situation with her rational mind. *Which told her she was in up to her neck and sinking.*

'You know, I think I'll enjoy being a married man.' He tucked her hand into the crook of his elbow and moved into the crowd on the footpath. 'It really will be a pleasure to get that side of my life settled. Now that I've taken the step, I don't know why I didn't do something about it ages ago.'

Claire's rational side was quickly elbowed aside by a very personal affront. *Ages ago? As in, before he'd even met her?*

It's all clinical to him. Given the circumstances, you should be grateful that's the way he feels about it.

She didn't feel grateful. She felt offended. Thoroughly hurt that he might have chosen some other woman and been just as happy about it.

You're not really marrying him, remember? It's all moot.

And this was exactly why she was going to end up in therapy.

Her fingers clenched around his forearm.

His muscles tensed in response, and that set the whole see-saw reaction in motion again. Desire, counter-desire. Emotional thrust, logical parry. She resisted the urge to tip her head back and yowl.

'I'm glad you're happy with your plans.' She murmured it in the blandest tone she could manage, and then pointed to a shopfront ahead of them, determined to distract herself. 'Have you ever been to Danny's Bakehouse? They serve a Jamaican Cheesecake Log that's to die for.'

And I could do with a slice right now. Or two. Or three. Scoffing cheesecake might not alter this situation, but it *would* suffuse it with a cheesecake-coated glow. That would surely be something positive?

'I haven't been there.' Nicholas turned his head to glance at the shop, and in that moment someone bumped her in the crush, jostling her against her boss's side.

An uneasy slither of tension climbed through her. She looked up, right into the gaze of the one person in the world she didn't want to see.

'Oops. Have to be careful these days.' He wore an ill-fitting suit over a slight paunch of a stomach. His balding head of hair was slicked back with something greasy. He ran a small photocopier repair business—and he was Sophie's blackmailer.

Gordon Haynes was a nondescript-looking man. He looked unthreatening. But when Claire searched his eyes, there was something dark and possibly unbalanced there that made her skin crawl.

This had to be a chance meeting. One that he was taking advantage of, but had not planned. She lifted her chin and stared him in those chilling eyes, refusing to let him rattle her. After the barest moment, when their gazes locked, he disappeared into the depths of the passing crowd and Claire breathed again.

'Are you all right?' Nicholas searched her face with his gaze. 'Did someone bump you?'

'I'm fine.' She squared her shoulders and forced the encounter from her mind. 'It was nothing.'

They made their way to the restaurant without further incident, and, once inside, quickly located the other couple and moved to join them.

'I should have asked for a potted history.' Claire's fingers tightened around her bag. 'Subjects I could raise with the wife, for starters.'

Nicholas's proposal had thrown her so far out of reality that she hadn't even considered how she would contribute to this lunch. She did now, and gave herself another opportunity to develop an ulcer.

'She lives for the marina, loves shopping and sailing.' Nicholas's response was calm. 'Don't worry about it. I'm sure you'll find something to talk about.'

'I'm just a little on edge right now.' The understatement made her feel slightly hysterical. She tried to maintain her poise as his hand moved to the small of her back to guide her through the maze of tables. It wasn't easy.

A little on edge? Try a lot!

They had always maintained a strict, impersonal relationship. Now all she seemed to want was his touch. His nearness. His heart, soul, and all the family secrets. He was giving her the touch and the nearness part, and was upsetting her equilibrium in the process.

And she should have been running a mile in the other direction. Doing her best not to even think about that side of things while she worked out just how she was going to get out of this crazy situation in one piece.

What if he wanted them to be intimate before the actual marriage? Feeling the way she did about him, how would she hold back? The more she thought about things, the more complications just seemed to keep coming.

'Naomi, Jack—may I introduce my assistant?'

In response to Nicholas's introductions, Claire nodded her hellos to the couple already seated at the restaurant table. 'Mrs Forrester, Mr Forrester.'

Nicholas held her chair. His hand brushed her nape as he stepped away to take his own seat. A mesmerising touch. She shivered, hot and cold at once. *That's right, Claire. You're doing a great job of staying calm and unruffled.*

'I hope you enjoyed smooth sailing?' Although Nicholas had addressed his comment to the other couple, and seemed absorbed in them, Claire sensed his continued awareness of her.

'A pleasant enough trip.' Jack Forrester had shrewd blue eyes set in a sun-weathered face, and looked to be somewhere in his early fifties. He winked at Claire in a jovial manner, but she sensed the sharpness of a keen mind behind the cheery façade. 'We like to take the opportunity to sail whenever we can.'

Claire wouldn't get out on the open sea for anything. She even avoided the harbour ferry whenever possible, sometimes at great inconvenience to herself. But she smiled dutifully back, determined not to do anything that might put this man off now that she had managed to stir an ember or two of work-related zeal back to life in herself.

The meal passed well enough, but Claire never lost her awareness of Nicholas, or of the numerous touches he managed to bestow on her.

Seriously. What if he wanted to make love on the office floor next? What would she do then?

Fall apart in his arms, most likely.

Maybe an affair wouldn't be so bad.

And maybe that's the stupidest thought you've ever had. You're holding out for love, remember? An emotion Nicholas doesn't even pretend to want to embrace.

Try telling her hormones that right at this moment. Try telling her heart. She groaned.

'Claire?'

At Nicholas's prompt, she turned. She hoped he hadn't read her lascivious thoughts. 'I'm sorry. What did you say?'

'Dessert has arrived.' He gestured towards the cart. 'Can I tempt you into something?'

Like bed, with a serving of loving kindness on the side?

Drat it, Claire. You have to stop thinking that way. Either way!

She ground her teeth. The other couple had already made their selections. A baked soufflé topped with a berry sauce for the husband, and a bowl of fruit salad for the wife. So innocuous. Why, then, did Claire find herself picturing Nicholas naked, nibbling soufflé and fruit salad from her navel?

I'll never see those foods in the same way again.

'The mixed sorbet,' she declared, and sucked in a shuddering breath.

Nicholas chose a platter of cheese and crackers, and to her great relief they settled to further discussion. She even managed to feel half in control of herself—until they reached the convivial stage and Nicholas draped his arm across her shoulders in casual possession.

Casual? *Ha.* One look at his face told her his thoughts exactly. She could no longer pretend any doubt in the matter. This was nothing casual, but all possession. His of her!

He ought to be careful. Next thing he knew, it would be *her* tossing *him* down on the office carpet so she could have her way with him.

There was something vividly erotic about a man playing games with the ends of one's hair, she found. And who was to say that a man couldn't be in lust first and then fall in love later?

'Would you pass me the water?' The request emerged as a strangled croak.

'Certainly.' He released her to reach for the carafe.

Great. She could breathe again. But then he leaned so close to her while he refilled her glass that she could smell the scent of his skin, could count the individual lashes that graced those enigmatic hazel eyes. Could feel the sensual tension emanating from him.

'Thank you,' she ground out.

He raised his eyebrows. 'You're welcome.'

She turned hastily away from him. 'Mr Forrester—Jack. How did you and Naomi build up your amazing empire? You've achieved incredible things with your properties and investments.'

Jack flirted a little with her as he answered, a born charmer, but Claire didn't think there was anything in it really. She smiled in a general sort of way, and encouraged him to elaborate about his various business ventures.

'Hard work, my dear.' Jack winked again, and leaned forward across the table as though to dispense a particularly juicy secret. 'If a man sets his mind to it, he can get pretty much whatever it is he wants in this life.'

'Not everything.' Nicholas's hand closed over Claire's shoulder in an almost painful grip. 'Some things are off limits.'

For the tiniest moment Forrester's gaze rested with shrewd, assessing sharpness on Nicholas. Then he laughed and toasted him with his coffee.

Naomi Forrester looked on in some bemusement. As well she might. Nicholas was acting like a possessive—well, boss-cum-fiancé. And Claire, although she definitely shouldn't have, liked it. She stifled a second groan.

The conversation wound up quickly after that, and they left the restaurant soon after.

Once clear of the building, Claire turned to Nicholas. 'Did we impress him? I couldn't tell.'

'We've made one more step with Forrester. For today, that's enough.' Nicholas settled Claire into the car and began the trip that would take them through the harbour tunnel and into the market suburb where he lived.

He could feel the tension pulling at his shoulders, and was disgusted with himself for it. All Forrester had done was flirt a bit with Claire, and Nicholas had wanted to separate the man's limbs piece by piece with his bare hands. *Caveman.*

He had to get control of this tendency to overreact about Claire. It was totally in contrast to the way he wanted to move their relationship forward. Calm, cool and unemotional. That was the plan.

'Forrester is the kind of man who enjoys watching his business associates go through hoops in an effort to snare him. He won't be easy to win.'

'I don't like that he's playing with you.' Claire seemed indignant, and Nicholas smiled. For all her intelligence and enthusiasm for her work, she was unaware of just how cutthroat the business world could be.

'*I'm* playing with *him*, too.' He shrugged. 'It's the way of it.' He tucked thoughts of the business lunch aside for examination later, and turned the subject to a matter that meant more to him at the moment. 'Before we go back to the office, I want to collect something from my house.'

'Oh, okay.'

Claire didn't have a lot else to say, but he didn't mind the quiet. It allowed him to reflect on the success of his plans so far. Four months from now—four months and two days, to be exact—they would be married. Despite that incident with the jealousy, which had been a simple glitch, he liked the idea of marrying Claire more and more.

When they arrived at the house, Claire gazed about with apparent interest. 'How long have you had a home here? I'd have pictured you in an apartment, to tell the truth.'

'I bought this place six years ago.' He swung the car into the driveway of a large two-storey home. Roman columns supported a porch that stretched the full width of the house on the lower storey. Above, a balcony circled around to the back.

The deep gold brick came from an Outback town that had the only kiln of its kind in Australia. Although the house wasn't modern in design, it was original, and it pleased him. He had an urge to try to convince Claire that she'd love it here, and squashed it. He didn't have to impress her.

'I thought you should see where you'll be living.'

'It's very nice.' She seemed sincere, but reluctant to say more, and quickly turned her attention to the flowerbeds.

Nicholas refused to acknowledge any sense of relief at her approving assessment.

'Those borders are pretty.' Claire gestured towards the blooming plants and bushes. 'I'm a closet gardener, you know. A frustrated one, at my apartment complex, but I'd have a great big garden if I had the opportunity.'

Was this what she'd meant by getting to know each other better? That they should share small, intimate details about each other?

He decided he could live with her revelations, and maybe come up with a few simple ones of his own. It wouldn't kill him to try, particularly if all they had to talk about were innocuous things like gardening. 'You can take over the care of the garden when we're married, if you like. Come and see the interior.'

Nicholas led the way to the front door, disarmed the security system, and stood back to allow her to precede him. 'We'll start upstairs and work our way down.'

He showed her the bedrooms, exchanging casual conversation with her as they made the tour. After the first few minutes she relaxed, and so, he found, did he. Claire *did* like his home, and there was nothing wrong with him feeling a bit of pride about that.

His feeling of ease left him abruptly when they stepped into the master bedroom. Her eyes turned to deep velvet brown, and a pink flush suffused her cheeks before she quickly looked anywhere but at him.

His pulse leaped, but he only said, 'The view is rather spectacular from here at night.' He threw the drapes open. 'That's one of the reasons the living room and kitchen are above stairs, rather than below. Would you like to see?'

'That would be nice.' She moved past him, the flags of colour in her cheeks still very much in evidence. 'It's a treat to see the harbour from a different perspective—although I appreciate the view of it from your office, too.'

Who cared about sights like the Opera House and Sydney Harbour Bridge? He wanted to ravish her, here and now. The temptation made him clench his hands as she passed him.

I'll have her in my bed when the time is right. Not because of some impulsive, and thoroughly controllable urge.

Anything else would smack of being driven, and nothing drove Nicholas Monroe to act in any way that he didn't first plan, then initiate in his own time.

'I could live out here.' Her words floated back to him, and he moved to join her on the balcony. 'You can see every bit of movement on the harbour so clearly.'

Their shoulders brushed, and he allowed himself to enjoy the scent of her, the warmth of her skin. 'The Forresters' yacht must be out there somewhere.'

'Yes, out there somewhere...' She sounded tense, and when his hip brushed hers she gasped. 'You could enclose this balcony, you know. Partially.' Her words ran into each other in a hasty jumble. 'Nothing to obscure the view, but you'd gain a little more privacy to sit out here. Imagine lying back in a Jacuzzi at the end of the day—' She stopped, an appalled look on her face.

'I can imagine it quite well.' His words were low-pitched, a counter to her staccato burst of nervous speech. He wanted her, and he wanted her to know it. 'A Jacuzzi made for two.'

'Uh, and potted plants.' She stepped away and positioned herself at the wrought-iron railing. 'There could be big banks of them all along here. Ornamental trees, and bamboo. Herbs. You could even grow strawberries.'

Nicholas thought about pushing, and decided against it. For now. In a way, this was no different from his game with Forrester, and Nicholas was a good and patient player. Yes. He liked thinking about it in those terms.

'Come down to the study. I want something from the safe, then we can head back to the office.'

She followed him with alacrity, apparently happy to go anywhere that took them away from bedrooms and talk of Jacuzzis.

He opened the safe and withdrew a large flat box. Inexplicably, his heart seemed to beat unevenly, and he couldn't quite draw a full breath. 'We'll choose the rings together, after we've given your sister the news.' He fingered the box, then handed it to her. 'I'm too well-known to hope someone wouldn't notice what we were doing and let the secret out. But these are for now.'

'Oh, but I can't.' She shot him a look of pure panic.

'I insist.' Her reticence left him somehow irritated. She should have jumped at the idea of a gift, as any woman would. His mother had certainly taken all his father could give her, and demanded even more. Jewels. New cars. Closets full of exotic clothes—so many she could never wear them all before they went out of fashion.

Nicholas would be able to afford Claire, no matter how expensive she turned out to be, but he wouldn't be held to ransom by her. Money she could have, but emotions would stay out of it. And the relationship would stay uncomplicated as a result. It was as simple as that—and if he had slipped a time or two today, that was simply because this was all new to him.

'Open it. Tell me what you think.'

For a moment he thought she might thrust the box back at him and run. Then, with trembling fingers, she lifted the hinged lid to reveal the matched set of diamond and gold jewellery inside. Drop necklace, choker, bracelet and earrings. All hand-crafted to his specifications by one of Sydney's most exclusive creative jewellers.

'These are Montichelli.' A soft gasp escaped her parted lips. 'The design…the gold leaves are tiny, but are they plane tree leaves?'

He nodded.

Claire let out a soft sigh. 'I've always loved those leaves, especially in spring, when they first emerge on the trees so fresh and green.'

'You made a comment about them the day you started working as my personal assistant.' He wondered why he was bothering to even mention it, and cleared his throat.

'And you remembered?' Her gaze flew to his face, panicky, overwhelmed.

Nicholas gave her a quelling look. 'It's no big deal, Claire. A random thought at the time, that's all.'

'Oh, well.' She glanced again at the jewellery, then back at his face. 'But you can't do this. I mustn't let you. They're beautiful, but—'

'Nonsense—no buts and ifs and maybes.' He took the box from her nerveless fingers and selected one of the pieces. 'I want to see you wearing these, Claire. You'll look good in all of it, but for today we'll start with the pendant.'

He pulled her forward and clasped the chain about her slender neck. The diamond nestled at the top of her breasts, surrounded by its leafy setting. She lifted her hand to touch the piece.

'Thank you.' Her mouth was soft, all womanly vulnerability. 'You'll probably never know what you've made me feel right now. I don't think I can tell you.'

There. That was the feminine reaction he had expected. Hang something expensive on her and she would act just like any other woman. Nothing compared to a pricey gift.

'I'm glad they please you.' He said it dismissively.

'Nicholas.' She clasped one hand to the back of his head and touched her lips to his.

Another typical feminine act. Except it was such a gentle touch, even as it made fire rage through his veins. He pulled her close, considering having that sexual satisfaction here and now, after all.

'I want you.' He let his mouth take hers, commanding her response and revelling in it when he got it. Other uneasy concerns were forgotten as the heat of the moment wrapped around him. Desire spiralled quickly. Her lips were soft, incredibly yielding, her mouth a tempting cavern, hot and lush. 'We're good together, Claire. You feel it too, don't you?'

She gasped and broke away, panting, her eyes widened with shock, awareness—and wanting. 'You won't go too fast for me?'

Right at this moment he wanted a rushed trip that led straight to the bedroom door, and beyond. But this was, after all, just about sex. It would wait for the next move in the game.

He swept up the jewellery case and caught her elbow with his other hand. 'Let's get back to work.'

'A good idea.' She drew a deep breath and squared her shoulders. 'Let's go back to the office.'

CHAPTER FOUR

CLAIRE'S edgy tension stayed with her the rest of the day. She couldn't stop thinking about the Montichelli jewellery. Although it might not have been his intention, Nicholas's choice of design, and his reasons behind it, had touched her deeply.

He wanted to be unemotional, yet he did things that seemed tailored specifically to make her react. When he touched her heart in that way Claire wanted desperately to believe that he was moved in similar fashion, but she knew he wasn't.

Then there had been that kiss back at his house. The sexual desire, she knew, would only be satisfied by complete surrender, but things were complicated enough already. Sleeping with Nicholas would only make them worse. Yet she had a suspicion that making love with her boss, if she was ever fortunate

74

enough to have him see it in that light, would be something above memorable.

'Nicholas...'

'Hmm?'

'Oh. Sorry.' She glanced at his profile, and away again. 'Was I muttering?'

'Sounded like it.'

He was driving her home, ostensibly to make sure her jewellery arrived safe and sound, and her along with it. He'd said he didn't want her to put herself at risk on the bus service, carrying that kind of cargo.

She welcomed the escort. She wanted to be able to return the jewellery safely to him later, even though it would kill her to part with it, but she wished he didn't have to see her very modest home. It seemed like an invasion, an exposure of herself that she would rather not allow.

'My apartment's in that building ahead on the left.' She pointed. 'The one with the brown brick mailboxes built into the wall.'

'I see.' His response gave nothing away. He simply pulled the car into the kerb and turned to her. 'Let's go.'

'I've been...ah...saving pennies for the future.' Saving to pay Sophie's blackmailer. 'The apartment isn't much.' A boring concrete square, decorated in beige everything. One among so many other concrete squares kitted out exactly the same.

It was cramped. The lift to the upper floors didn't work half the time. Suddenly her chin came up. She was officially a clerical pool worker, after all. She might be living a little poorly, but at least she had no aspirations above her station.

You don't call agreeing to marry your millionaire boss as having thoughts beyond reality?

Her mouth pursed. She wasn't going to marry him. She was simply buying time. And that was his fault anyway. She refused to blame herself for it. Now, if only her overwrought nerves would agree with her, and she could ignore her emotional reactions for a while!

'I'm afraid you'll find my flat rather drab.'

'My father wasn't a wealthy man, Claire.' His tone held an edge. 'And what he had he didn't always spend wisely. I do understand the meaning of cash constraints.'

Claire knew nothing of the real details of Nicholas's upbringing, other than that he had a couple of brothers and his father owned a construction company of some kind in Brisbane. His mother was a physiotherapist and Reiki healer, and his parents were divorced.

Family life wasn't always happy, or necessarily comfortable, a fact Claire knew only too well herself.

Nicholas had built his empire from nothing, she knew that much, and she wondered now if his childhood lack had driven him to achieve such success. She heaved a sigh, took a firm grip on the jewellery case, and led the way indoors.

The lift actually worked for a change. She supposed she should be thankful for small mercies, but as they stepped inside and the doors rumbled closed the contraption lurched and threw her into Nicholas's arms.

In an instant, his mouth covered hers. The lift smoothed out, but her world continued to tilt. He sent her out of control so easily it was frightening. Then Nicholas broke away and turned to face the door, almost as though nothing had happened or as though he wished it hadn't.

'Why did you do that?' Was she asking why he had kissed her, or why he had stopped? She wasn't sure. 'I don't know what to do with you in this mood.'

'No need to worry.' He continued to stare straight ahead, but he was panting slightly, as though he had run hard and stopped suddenly. His tone harshened. 'I can always show you, if I think you need some instruction.'

'I wouldn't need showing.' She bit down on further words. This was no time to feel indignant. It was a relief to reach her floor and step out of the confined space. 'Here we are. Mine's fourth from the end—number twenty two.'

'Give me the key, Claire. I'll open up for you.'

It felt intimate to enter the little apartment together. As though they were…an old married couple. There was a part of her that yearned for a sense of belonging, for a link with someone special.

In other circumstances it would have thrilled her for Nicholas to be that person. But now she had to keep her feelings closed off from him. A sense of family and togetherness was not something he would encourage. If only she could get all this firmly in her mind and keep it there.

Inside the flat, he looked around with interest. The interlude in the lift was, apparently, something to be quickly forgotten. By him, at least.

'I like this. It has a certain charm about it.'

She eyed him suspiciously, but he seemed sincere. 'I've tried to make a home out of it.' She moved into the tiny living room and fluffed one of the throw cushions on the small sofa. 'The furnishings are a mishmash. A few special things from my parents' home, that I kept after they died, the rest I've picked up at rummage sales, mostly, or bought second hand and refurbished by myself.'

'You've done a good job.' He paused. 'Coffee might be nice.' The suggestion held a note of...appreciation?

'I don't understand.' She swept a pile of gardening magazines aside on the coffee table, and laid the jewellery case down. 'Why are you—'

'Impressed?' He glanced around him again. 'Show me where you sleep, Claire. I want to see it.'

It wasn't an invitation to sexual intimacy, although she had the impression that particular beast was only slumbering. 'It's not hard to find. It's the only other room aside from the bathroom.'

He stood back to let her open the door to the second tiny room, then pushed her through it and followed. Silence reigned as he looked his fill. It seemed to take for ever and she still couldn't understand the expression on his face. All she knew was the yearning in her own soul.

It was intense, and it crept through her with the stealth of a cat slinking through the shadows at midnight. She wanted him to sense her presence here, be attracted to the heart of her that had gone into the room.

Their gazes locked. Claire's emotions shuddered and rocked, swelling inside her. Suddenly it was all intense after all. They should get out of the confined space. Right now.

'The coffee,' she said. 'I should get it.'

'In a minute.' He touched the tips of his fingers to the red ruffled pillow covers on the bed. Ran a hand across the maroon and gold spread. 'You favour bright colours.'

'Sometimes.' Not for the office. There she wanted to project efficiency and control, and those qualities seemed to look their best in muted shades. At home, bright colours lifted the atmosphere. Gave it depth. Cheered her up.

'You've breathed life into all this.' He indicated their surroundings with a single, expressive sweep of his hand. 'You've made it your own.'

'Isn't that what should be done with a home, be it ever so humble?'

'I want you in *my* home, like this.'

Claire's foolish heart leapt, but immediately he spoke, a fierce frown descended over his face.

'Actually, a decorator would be a better idea.' He turned and left the room. 'Do I get that coffee?'

'Uh, sure. But it'll only be instant.' She led the way to the kitchenette end of the living room, disappointed that she had misread his mood so thoroughly, even though none of it would make a difference in the end. 'I don't do the real stuff.'

He drank his coffee standing up, in less than two minutes, in silence. The atmosphere thickened with whatever it was he was choosing not to say.

Finally, he plonked the coffee mug down on the bench. 'It's time I left.'

She walked with him to the door, and paused there. 'Goodnight, Nicholas.'

Something in her heart continued to ache, but she told herself it couldn't be anything worse than indigestion. After all, given their circumstances, she knew better than to develop real feelings for him.

Still, she wouldn't have minded the chance to lay her head against his shoulder and forget the rest of her life for a moment. Maybe even to give a little comfort in return. Was such a small scrap too much to want? She knew the answer, of course.

'You shouldn't have given me the jewellery, but I'll wear it whenever you want me to.'

'Goodnight, Claire.' He brushed his lips against hers and stepped out into the corridor. Then he stopped and snapped his fingers, a man very clearly in control of himself and his world. 'One other thing. I hope your weekend is free.'

She stared at him, bemused more by the casual bussing of her mouth than by his words. 'Why?'

'Because we'll be spending it on Brandmeire Island.'

'Brandmeire?' She felt like an idiot, simply repeating the name, but her brain refused to compute his statement. 'That's where you're going with the Forresters and their other guests.'

The trip would provide another step forward in his effort to snare the Forrester account. Claire was happy for Nicholas, but the retreat at one of the small islands off the Queensland coast had nothing to do with her.

Other than that in other circumstances it would have provided an unforgettable weekend to add to a store of romantic moments. But since Nicholas didn't do romance, and this engagement wasn't as real as he thought anyway, she wished he would stop putting these tempting ideas into her head.

'Exactly.' He pulled her forward and kissed her to the point of fiery heat, then set her back inside the door. 'You're coming, too. Make sure you pack to play, as well as for work. I'm sure there'll be time to do both, and I plan to make the best use of that time.'

The words held a sensual promise as unmistakable as the life force of his kiss. And both warned her, in no uncertain terms.

No way in the wide world should she go on a work-and-play weekend with Nicholas. Not if she wanted to stay out of his arms—and his bed. And certainly not if she wanted to stop the tide of feeling he seemed to have unleashed in the deepest heart of her.

She hadn't asked for any of this, and now that it was happening her feelings had turned into her enemy. She hadn't even realised she *had* some of these cravings until Nicholas had made it clear she couldn't give in to them with him.

'You don't want me there for something like that. I'm sure the Forresters and the others won't want an interloper, either.'

'You're not an interloper. They think you're my girlfriend, and you're coming along.' He raised a haughty brow. 'Unless you have a problem with the idea of our spending time getting to know each other? You did say you needed that.'

'Yes.' She narrowed her gaze in deliberate warning. 'Time is exactly what I need.'

What she really needed was to get out of this mess without intimacy deepening any further—on any level. And she couldn't get out until she had paid the last installment to the blackmailer. A whole three months more, and then she'd still have to call off the wedding after that.

'I don't mind the idea of going away, I suppose, it's simply that I—'

'Good. Then that's settled. We'll leave work a bit earlier tomorrow afternoon, swing by here to collect your things, then head for the airport.' With a quick salute, he turned and strode away.

—won't sleep with you under any circumstances, she completed silently.

'Lock up, Claire.' His words floated back to her.

'Pardon? Oh, I was about to.' She banged the door shut with more force than necessary, and for good measure shot the bolt home with a satisfying thwack. She wasn't sure just who or what she was angry at, really. But, whatever the cause, this reaction had to be better than despair.

'I won't go away with him, and that's that.' She made the declaration as she flung herself onto the sofa in preparation for the think-time she had promised herself. 'I'll claim to have come down with the flu or something, and spend the weekend curled up in bed, catching up on my reading. That will show him.'

Friday dawned bright and cheery, which didn't match Claire's outlook at all. Despite her efforts to think through her situation, she had gone to bed no clearer about how to keep out of trouble for the next three months than she had been before she started.

When her alarm went off, she dithered, panicked, stressed, and finally called in to say she was sick. Nicholas saw straight through her, and told her to hurry and get to work. They had a lot to do before they could leave.

He sounded happy. Happier than she had ever heard him. Had *she* given him that with her marriage agreement? And, if so, how would he handle it when she pulled the plug before the ceremony?

She didn't want to hurt him. Didn't believe he was able to *be* hurt. But what if she was wrong?

You're not wrong. He's not into emotions. You're letting your imagination carry you away. Now, stop worrying—before you drive yourself right around the twist.

The working day behind them, they were now airborne on their way to Brandmeire, and Claire was no more certain of anything. Herself, her feelings, how she was going to get through the next minute, let alone the next day or three months.

'Feeling okay?' Nicholas searched her face with a look that, on the surface at least, appeared solicitous. 'You're not scared of small aircraft, I hope?'

'I rarely get scared.' *Except when my life is spiralling out of control before my eyes.*

Her statement smacked of irony, anyway, given that she had tried to pretend illness to get out of this trip. He had said a few swift words on the subject when she'd got to work. Had pointed out that he had no intention of ravishing her the first opportunity he got.

Huh. Hot and cold. Going after her with fire in his eyes one minute, then telling her he couldn't care less the next. *He* certainly wasn't stressed. He looked the epitome of relaxation in his casual trousers and shirt, his hair a little mussed from their windblown departure from the city airport.

It made her want to scream—or throw something. She pretended uninterest instead. 'I'm okay. Small planes don't bother me.'

She fingered the diamond bracelet on her wrist, tracing the gold leaf design lovingly, and wondered what Nicholas would think if she told him she had slept with the box of jewellery hidden beneath her mattress last night.

'Is the jewellery insured?' she blurted into the silence.

'Yes, Claire.' He glanced at her wrist, a measure of humour in his expression. 'The jewellery is insured.'

His amusement only served to aggravate her more. When she spoke, she didn't try to hide her belligerence. 'I'd still rather keep it all in the office safe, or in the one at your house.'

'If you did that you'd rarely wear it.' He made the point with irrefutable logic. 'That would somewhat defeat the purpose of the exercise.'

That depends on whose purpose we're talking about, Claire thought. *It would suit my purpose rather well.*

'That's Brandmeire below.' Nicholas was cheerfully calm. A confident man in a wrinkle-free world. 'We should be landing soon.'

'So I see.' She made a show of watching the expanse of rippling blue ocean come up to meet them.

An island paradise. Her boss. And a whole weekend looming ahead like one long, endless opportunity for disaster.

This is not a romantic interlude. There will be no memory-building done on this trip.

She had been repeating the mantra on and off all day, but somehow there was a wayward part of her that simply didn't want to believe it. A part that looked at Nicholas and saw the potential for so many unspoken, longed-for things.

She sighed. 'I could take a dip in that ocean right about now.'

Like, throw myself off the nearest pier and take my chances with the sharks. I doubt they'd be any more threatening than the thoughts teeming about inside my head right at this moment.

Thoughts of kissing her boss, of touching and holding him in ways she had no business thinking about. And that was the least of it. He might have said he wasn't after seduction this trip, but did he really mean it? Worse, did she *want* him to mean it, even at the risk of getting herself into a deeper tangle?

'We'll definitely spend some time in the water this weekend.' A smile of anticipation lifted Nicholas's sensual mouth. 'I love swimming, and I'm not about to miss the opportunity to enjoy the sight of my future wife in a swimsuit, either.'

'I suppose I should check you out, too,' she snapped back, aggravated, and—yes, okay—a little bit excited by his blatant interest in her body. She was angry with herself for being so. Why should her *heart* leap, in response to a purely *bodily* reference? 'You do wear swimming briefs, I hope? Not all-concealing board shorts?'

For a moment his expression froze, then he threw back his head and laughed. 'Touché, Claire. Touché.'

The plane touched down, and jolted several times before it settled to a steady taxi along the runway. All too soon they had dispatched the formalities, collected luggage, and been deposited outside an ultra-modern glass and timber bungalow that had the sea practically lapping at its foundations.

The place looked romantic, of course. All sleek, sun-beaten wood and shiny see-through panes. Indeed, the entire island was a veritable paradise.

Claire tried to visualise herself outside the bungalow door, seated at a desk in her working clothes, with a notebook perched on her knees.

Businesslike, she chanted to herself. *Business, business, business.*

'Is the bungalow for me or for you?' She tried to sound calm, cheerful, as though they hadn't recently clashed wills. As though she wasn't a jumble of confusion inside. Not to mention her rioting hormones. Noticing that her shoulders were tense, she deliberately relaxed her pose. 'It looks very nice. I thought we might have rooms in the resort hotel, but one of these would be good, too. Not that I would mind the hotel.'

She was actually reduced to babbling. On that thought, she snapped her mouth shut.

Nicholas's lips twitched. 'The cabin is for both of us. Let's go in and unpack. We'll have about enough time for that, and a drink, before we have to change and head over to the hotel for an evening with the Forresters and the others.'

'I thought I'd made it clear I won't sleep with you this weekend.' When he didn't respond, simply looked at her with one brow irritatingly lifted, she ploughed on. 'In fact, I have very strong feelings about the sanctity of marriage altogether. A bride should wait for her husband. For the wedding night.'

There had to be some women who still thought that way. She might have herself if she hadn't been so attracted to Nicholas that she struggled even to string two thoughts together in his presence. But she had to take a stand on this, so she threw back her head and stared him down with the steeliest expression she could muster.

'Are you a virgin, Claire? If so, there's nothing to be scared about, you know. Sex was made to be enjoyed.' His voice dropped to a deep, intimate rumble. 'Between us, I know it will be very enjoyable.'

'I know that.' A fiery heat swarmed up her neck and into her face. 'I mean, I know I don't have to be scared of sex. I've done it.'

Not that it was particularly great that one time, but that's not the point.

'I'm talking about what my feelings are *now*,' she said. 'And *now* I want to wait for the marriage.'

For the marriage that isn't ever going to happen. I'm trying to keep things uncomplicated here, Nicholas, and you're not helping a whole lot.

'When it's right for us to make love, we'll make love.' He took her suitcase from her, lifted his into his other hand, and stepped inside. 'I doubt you'll want to wait for the wedding night. There's way too much awareness between us for that. But I guess time will tell.'

Make love. If only.

'You can't just force me into your bed and have your way with me, you know.' The idea made a wholly improper surge of anticipation skim along her pulse-points. 'This isn't some situation with a—a—a Neanderthal man dragging off his mate by her hair. I tell you, I'm a modern woman. I understand my rights, and I know some karate, too. Don't think I won't use everything I know. I won't co-operate, even if you throw me down forcibly and—'

'Why don't you choose a room?' He dumped the suitcases on the floor and strode across the tiled living room to flick a switch on the air-conditioning unit. 'Unpack your things, then we'll have that drink I promised and get ready to head across to the hotel.'

'Choose a room?'

As in one of the two rooms. As in he had no intention of forcing her to do anything. He wasn't even inviting her, for heaven's sake. Mortification spread all over her like a rash.

'Right. I'll, uh, I'll do that. I'll go and, um, choose a room.'

Was it possible to suffer death by embarrassment? Claire felt close to finding out!

CHAPTER FIVE

'DRINK?' Nicholas turned from the bar-fridge as Claire stepped out of her room. She wouldn't quite meet his gaze.

Ignoring her unease—it had been with her all evening, ever since she'd told him they wouldn't be making love this weekend on Brandmeire—he told her the selection.

'After all that schmoozing tonight, I think we deserve one.'

'This might still be the same Friday we started in Sydney this morning, but an island off the coast is a very different setting to the Monroe building. This evening didn't seem much like work.' Her cream calf-length skirt swished against her legs as she left the doorway and moved towards him. 'Or maybe standing around eating canapés and drinking cocktails was the reason. Do you think you made an impression on the Forresters?' she added. 'I swear I'm beginning to really dislike

96

that man, and the way he plays people off each other for his own amusement.'

'It's his nature.' Nicholas didn't like it either, but he gave a philosophical shrug. With another part of him he examined the way Claire's eyes sparkled. She'd had just enough wine to put a bit of a flush in her cheeks, to make her look as if she was seeing nothing but stars.

She was spectacular. Want drove through him on a sudden burst. *Forrester. This discussion is about business—remember?*

'I'll give him his weekend of amusement, but by the end of it he'll know I'm serious, and that I won't wait around for a decision from him for ever. There are always other fish to fry.'

Claire gave him an approving look as she waved an arm towards the fridge. 'Actually, I'm not sure if I need another drink. But thanks for the offer.'

He shut the fridge and tried not to think about that swirling skirt, or the long, luscious legs beneath it. He was only human, after all, despite his declaration that he had no intention of pushing things with her. Those possessive urges had been playing him up again, too, particularly around the flirting Jack Forrester. This continued reaction made Nicholas uncomfortable with himself in a way he wasn't used to.

'What about coffee, then?'

'No.' She folded her arms around her middle. 'I probably should just go to… Uh, I should just turn in for the night.' She paused, and the gentle colour in her cheeks turned into a deep, rosy display. 'I'm embarrassed about the way I behaved earlier. I owe you an apology for jumping to conclusions the way I did. I'm—well, I'm sorry. I feel pretty stupid about it right now.'

'You were strung up.'

She still was—stretched tighter than the catgut on a violin, in fact. He had managed to overlook that while she was high on the exhilaration of the evening, but it was as clear as crystal to him now.

'I'm not out to make things difficult for you, Claire, or to push you in directions you're not ready for. If you can just believe that, I think things will go a lot easier for you.'

Maybe if they both thought that, this baffling inner tension would leave *him*, as well.

'The way I carried on, you must think I'm a real wuss. But I'm not.' She bent to take off her shoes, and flung them through the open door into her room. 'For every choice I make there's a reason, although it may not seem that way at times.'

He should keep his distance, but he couldn't resist. It was almost as though something inside was driving him, forcing him to act outside his will. He reached out and clasped her shoulders.

'You don't have to justify your choices to me, Claire.'

If she knew his thoughts she might not be so inclined to do so, either. He wanted to make love with her, and damn her principles and everything else. He even wondered if his own principles were at stake. Certainly he had never felt this antsy kind of unease before.

'You're short without your shoes.'

His observation brought a glare to her face. It also distracted her from her embarrassment, as he had intended, and distracted *him* from his confusing thoughts.

'Am not.' She drew a deep breath and straightened to her full height. 'I'll have you know I stand at a hundred and seventy centimetres in my stockinged feet. I believe that's five foot eight in imperial measurements—in case you're too old to be comfortable with metric.'

He laughed. 'I see the cat has claws.'

'Take *your* shoes off, then.' Militant sparks lit her eyes. 'We'll see how tall you think you are once we're on an even playing field.'

'I think I'll end up with the greatest advantage.' He indicated the shoes tossed on the floor of the room behind them. 'The heels on those things must be close to fifteen *centimetres.*'

'Huh!' She folded her arms again.

Nicholas wished she wouldn't. Her black top was form-fitting enough to keep his blood pressure on high alert without any additional help. Talk about regressing to your most uncivilised origins. He didn't want any other man to even *see* her when she looked like this. But at least his mind was off the rollercoaster ride of his recent thoughts.

'I'll take my shoes off for a walk along the beach,' he offered. They could probably both do with a few minutes outside. In his case to cool his libido, and whatever else it was that had him so stirred up. 'What do you say?'

Her gaze moved to the glass panelling behind him, and she gave a wry smile. 'Do you know how rare it is for me to get to the beach? *Any* beach—let alone a paradise like this one?'

He toed his shoes off and bent to remove his socks. 'Then you should enjoy these surroundings while you can.'

'You've convinced me.' Her smile was almost relaxed. 'Let's take a walk.'

The sand looked white in the moonlight, and was cool beneath their feet. With the lap of the waves to their left, and the lush tropical foliage joining the beach on the right, they were completely secluded.

It was a romantic spot, Nicholas thought. The kind of place for sharing something really special. He cringed when he realised how he had allowed his thoughts to slip into such foolish whimsy.

'There doesn't seem to be anyone else about.' Claire moved further over to walk in the shallows. 'I'd have thought a few people would be out here enjoying this.'

'Most of them are probably still up at the hotel, indulging in the entertainment.' Or ensconced in their cabins or rooms, making their own.

They fell into silence and just walked. Claire seemed content to breathe the sea air and dabble in the shallows of the water. Now and again, when a deeper wave rolled in, she would run back up the beach. Occasionally they passed another couple, but for the most part the beach remained deserted.

Nicholas was content for Claire to be content. Another worrying development? No. There was nothing wrong with wanting her to be happy.

She gave a soft laugh into the silence.

'What is it?' He turned to examine her face in the moonlight. Her hair flowed around her shoulders, caressing her face in gentle curls. In the darkness, her eyes were deep, mysterious pools. He had the weirdest urge to dive into them and lose himself.

'You'll think it's silly. I was just wondering how early a person would have to rise to find the best seashells before anyone else got to them.' She smiled. 'Childish, huh?'

Not if it was what she wanted to do. This time the turn of his thoughts barely even registered.

'Must be the moonlight,' he muttered.

'Hmm?'

Her dreamy response made him want to tug her close, so he could feel her warmth against his chest as they strolled. 'There's a spot on the other side of the island that's good for shells. They don't come in much here.'

'You've been here before?' She paused to look at him. 'I hadn't realised.'

'I came a few years ago, with my brothers and my dad. We try to catch a weekend away together a couple of times a year.'

'I envy you those relationships.' She sounded wistful.

He almost opened his mouth and told her she would be able to share them, before he realised—*again*—that he had allowed himself to get off track. Instead, he reached out to brush a strand of hair from her face.

He shouldn't have touched her, though, because now he wanted to do it again—and to do more. 'We should head back. It must be getting late.'

'Time to snare some beauty sleep.' She agreed readily enough, but her gaze roved his face, hovering here and there, while a pulse throbbed at the base of her neck.

Nicholas wanted to kiss the golden skin there. Instead, he captured her hand in his and headed back the way they had come. When they reached the cabin, he led her inside, and let go. 'You can use the bathroom first. Goodnight.'

'Goodnight, Nicholas.' She leaned up to brush a kiss against his lips. 'You've been very understanding. No matter what happens, I won't forget that.'

The words were almost vehement. Her gaze searched his face, and he knew by her expression that she wanted to kiss him again. He forgot about his sense of confusion. Forgot everything but how much he wanted this.

'Do it,' he charged softly, and she closed her eyes and leaned closer. But it was he who swooped, who took her lips and plundered in just the way he had told himself he wouldn't.

Claire did that to him, and the knowledge made him uncomfortable. It was dangerous to give her any control over him. Look how he was starting to change already, despite his determination not to.

It wasn't love. Of course not. But she was having some sort of effect on him that he hadn't anticipated. He should take that as a warning to be very, very careful. Yet he didn't want to stop this. Not right now, anyway.

His arms closed about her shoulders, locking her to him. 'Kiss me again.'

'I will. I am.' She met him again, wound her arms around his neck and pressed close.

Much of her shoulders were bare to his touch. He kissed the slight tang of the sea from her mouth and ran his palms over soft, satiny skin. 'Open your mouth for me. Let me inside.'

'Lord, *Nicholas*.'

She opened, he plunged, and their tongues mated and tangled, exploring each other, learning. Blood pounded through his veins. His arms locked tighter around her. The pressure was good, but he still wanted more.

More touching her, holding her, and something even more still. Something that might soothe the rawness that he felt inside.

Her hands slipped to his shoulders, and to his chest. He groaned, clenching his muscles against the tide of pleasure and wanting. His hands swept over her. Spine. Hips. Arms. Shoulders. And down to cup the globes of her bottom through the skirt, pressing her against his need.

In another moment he would lift her, carry her to his bed. To bring them together in every way possible seemed the only thing that mattered.

But if he did that he would be completely out of control. Not just mostly, as he was now.

The thought doused him like icy water, and the effect was as dramatic. Shaking—*shaken*—

he pulled back from her. Almost harshly, he thrust her from him.

'Think about us while you lie alone tonight.' He turned away. 'Ask yourself why you're determined to put off making love together, when it's clear you want it. Sex and companionship, Claire.' It did him good to remind himself of it, too. 'That's where we're headed. Why wait?'

Claire's agonised, muffled groan filled his ears as he stepped into his room and closed the door. But it was his own unease that went with him. What was she doing to him to make him feel so desperate for her? Now that he was away from her, able to clear his head a little, he reminded himself that this reaction to her was intolerable. Unacceptable. No part of his plans.

Other reactions were more predictable, but they, too, demanded his notice. He gave his bed a single dismissive glance, pulled a sheaf of paperwork out of his briefcase, and slammed his fraught body into a cane chair in the corner.

If there was to be any sleep for him tonight, he suspected it wouldn't come soon.

CHAPTER SIX

THE audience with Jack Forrester—and *audience* was definitely the way Claire saw the man's agreement to a meeting with Nicholas on Saturday morning—was as frustrating as their previous interactions.

When they emerged from the room, Claire was fuming. Anger sparked in her veins and loosened her tongue. The man had been positively *rude* to Nicholas. It was totally intolerable!

'Aren't you annoyed? He seemed to barely listen to you half the time. Where does he think he gets off, treating the head of Monroe's that way? You're brilliant. You made a great presentation, and Monroe's is the best he'll get. What's his problem? I'm glad you let him know you won't wait around for ever for him.'

When her tirade had ended, she closed her mouth in surprise. Nicholas had butted heads with other businessmen plenty of times in the

108

past, but this was the first time Claire had wanted to tear his opponent apart as a result.

Great. Now she could add Mama Bear Syndrome to her other problems. *You touch Papa Bear, and I'll take this furry paw and cuff you all the way into next week with it.*

'Don't worry about it. The meeting served its purpose. Now we wait to see what happens next—and I, for one, plan to enjoy the rest of my weekend here.' He smiled as he stuffed the last of his papers into his briefcase and strode up the corridor. 'Aside from turning up to dinner tonight and a golf game tomorrow, I'm free to do what I want from now on.' His gaze rested on her with sudden intensity. 'How do you want to spend the afternoon, Claire?'

'Ah...a whole afternoon?' The perfect way to spend the time dropped into her thoughts, and heated her blood. Unfortunately it seemed to be *all* she could think of lately, since that explosive kiss.

Making love might seem the perfect idea, but in fact it would be nothing short of disaster. Make love. Hand Nicholas her heart on a plate. What was the difference? Easy. *There was none.*

'I don't know. I guess I'd like to explore more of the island.' That should be safe enough, shouldn't it?

Yes. As safe as wandering in an idyllic getaway with a man who abhorred romance yet made her feel warm and fuzzy all over just by being himself could ever be.

Nicholas quickly made their needs known to the resort staff, then turned to her. 'Let's go back to the cabin. Change clothes. They'll bring a Jeep to us there.'

Nicholas proved an able guide, and disarmed her when he remembered her interest in seashells. *See? He was doing it again. Being nice and making her feel all mushy in the no-go emotional zone.*

They examined hundreds of shells on a little piece of secluded beach on the opposite side of the island, with the tropical sun caressing its warmth onto them from above.

It was fun, actually. Enough so that Claire forgot to be uptight for a little while and just relaxed.

Nicholas, she discovered, was fun to relax *with*. He made silly quips that forced her to laugh. Led her along the sand as though she were a pre-schooler let loose for the afternoon. Just generally made her feel good. It might have been shortsighted, but she decided she would live for the moment, would let herself enjoy this little piece of fun and worry about the rest of her life again later.

'These are wonderful.' She rinsed another small shell in the surf and dropped it into a plastic bag with the others. 'I'd better stop collecting, though. Otherwise I'll sink through the sand from the weight of them all.'

'Time for a swim, then.' He spoke blandly enough, but his gaze challenged her and brought a sexual edge back into the day. 'You do have a suit on under that dress, I hope?'

'Ah, I do.' Her heart pounded with a mixture of awareness and dread. The latter was quite real, and for once had nothing to do with her boss or her hormones. 'But actually I don't swim in the sea. I only paddle.'

'Excuses, Claire?' He shook his head and turned to strip off his shirt and trousers and drop them on the sand. 'Come on. It's too nice a day to waste time. I promise I won't ogle you too much.'

She heard the teasing tone, but her gaze remained on the expanse of ocean. So innocent when she dabbled at its edge. So threatening further in.

'I don't swim in the sea. I'm not joking or trying to have an argument. It's simply a fact. I'll join you, and I'll go in up to my thighs. That's it.' She couldn't have committed to more at gunpoint.

It was all she could do not to beg him to stay in the shallows with her. She could imagine how well that would go down, but right now her newly discovered mother bear instincts were tangling with her fears. The result? She wanted Nicholas right where she could watch over him, thanks.

That wasn't going to be an option. She knew that, and strove to put on a calm front.

Nicholas would swim; she would dabble in the shallows. It would all be okay, and that was that.

She pulled her sleeveless dress up over her shoulders and head, and tossed it on top of his clothes on the sand. Only then did she look his way, and she had to stifle a gasp at the sheer physical beauty of him.

His shoulders were broad and muscled, his chest firm, with a smattering of curly black hair that narrowed to a vee on the way to his trim waist. The swimming briefs did little to disguise his masculine shape. She quickly dropped her gaze to the strong legs, then raised it back to his face. Only to find he was looking at her, too.

'You're perfect.' His praise was simple, but his gaze on her was hot, heady, as it travelled over her, lingering on her breasts, her hips, the length of her legs. 'I think that outfit is even more provocative than a bikini.'

The one-piece suit was red, streamlined, high-cut at the thighs, and cupped her breasts firmly. She had thought it perfectly sedate until his hot gaze bored through it to the flesh beneath. Her breasts tingled in response to him, and she turned quickly away. Maybe a dunking wouldn't be such a bad idea, after all.

'Last one in and all that.'

Claire didn't venture in far. Just waded while Nicholas went further out. He rode the waves, his dark head bobbing confidently in the water.

She clenched her fists at first, worrying about him, wanting to call him back, but she eventually convinced herself he was as confident at taming the waves as he was at everything else. He would be okay. It was a calm day, he knew what he was doing, and he wasn't in any danger here.

'Come out with me, Claire. I'll look after you.' He spoke from right beside her.

At the sound of his voice she jumped and shook her head. 'I'm happy here.'

'Happy? Or scared silly?' He flicked the hair back off his forehead and took her hand in a firm grip. 'I'll hold onto you the whole time, but you have to face this. You can't live in a harbour city the way you do and stay terrified of the water. It's crazy.'

He looked so confident and reassuring she almost believed him. Almost, but not quite.

'I'm not terrified.' The rest of her words died away as he tugged her close. So close that their bodies melded from chest to hip. Their legs entwined in a sensual dance and he led her further out into the water.

Bam went her thought-processes, her objections, any hint of coherency at all. Her fear was overridden by her awareness of his nearness. The tang of salt water meshed with the scent of his sun-warmed skin, turning her senses to liquid fire.

Before she knew it they were out of standing depth, bobbing up and down on the ebb and flow of the waves. Claire couldn't believe she was letting this happen.

'The current is gentle here.' He spoke softly, his gaze roving her face. 'Feel it. All you need to do is move with it, ride it.' He took her arms and wrapped them around his shoulders, his touch a fiery caress. 'Just as I long for you to ride me.'

Her legs had gone automatically around his waist in a panicked reaction that now became wholly erotic. Dear Lord, what was she doing? What was Nicholas doing to *her*?

Despite herself, she pressed closer, embracing the danger of the ocean and the danger of Nicholas, only two flimsy layers of cloth away from her.

A wave lifted them, buoyed them up, and they pressed nearer as his mouth lowered to cover hers. His hands pressed her spine until her chest flattened against his, her nipples rasping in sensitive awareness against her swimsuit, against his chest.

Claire forgot the sea. Forgot trying to keep her distance from Nicholas. Forgot her troubles, her concerns—everything but the feel of him, so right against her as his tongue probed the depths of her mouth, learning her, sweeping her away on a tide of longing, of rising need.

They were moving into shallower water. She scarcely noticed it until she realised he had stopped, had planted his feet firmly on the seabed. The water lapped over them at chest level and he continued to mesmerise her with his mouth, with his hands, and his hard, strong body.

He groaned, rocking against her, and she pressed closer, wanting him. Needing him. A moment later he lowered the straps of her swimsuit and pushed them down until her breasts were exposed to his gaze, to his touch.

'Look at you. So beautiful. So exquisite. Let me touch you, Claire.'

'Yes.' She groaned the word, desperate for it. Her nails grazed his back as he lifted his hands to cup her. The slide of his fingers sent roll after roll of sensation right to the heart of her.

She wanted to touch him, too, to be able to hold him close and never let him go. Slowly she unlocked her legs, sliding against him until they were both standing. Until her hand could reach tentatively to stroke his chest, his waist, and the hard, throbbing mound beneath his swimsuit. He came alive beneath her touch, groaned and swept her close, pressing kisses all over her face and shoulders in a heated rush.

'Claire, I want you so much.' He panted between each gasping word, his chest heaving.

Claire wanted him, too, wanted him with an ache that consumed her whole body and probably all of her soul. Every part of her cried out for him, for the fulfilment he would give her. This was nothing like that first, fumbling experience years ago, which had left her bewildered and wondering what all the fuss was about.

Her eyes opened. A slow, languorous sweep of her lashes that brought her gaze to his intimate, stroking green-flecked one. Green like the ocean, or the expanse of lush foliage at their backs.

At the thought, her eyes widened. Her gaze flew to his and glanced away, over her shoulder, to the deserted beach behind. They stood in the middle of the sea, where any passerby could observe them.

She didn't want observers. Didn't want this at all. Or at least couldn't let herself have it, even though she craved it. Shock and withdrawal set in. Her body began to tremble with an entirely different reaction, and she pushed at his shoulders, wedging distance between them like a shield.

'Not this way.'

It was all she could grind out between her chattering teeth. It wasn't what she meant to tell him at all, but the passion in his eyes banked, and he, too, looked towards the beach.

'No. Not this way. Not now. Go paddle in the shallows.' The muscles in his face were granite-hard as he held himself in check. 'I'll come out in a minute.'

After his swim, after she had made an attempt to calm herself, they ate. A picnic meal on the beach, thoughtfully provided by Nicholas for her comfort and enjoyment. Another romantic touch that he would vehemently deny if she tried to thank him for it on those terms.

She had no idea what she put in her mouth, or what she said. She knew only that her gaze couldn't meet his. That tension lay between them like a live thing, waiting to consume them both with greedy hands and fists and un-relenting passion.

The sun caressed her, drying her skin, but it couldn't warm away the chill of separation. Of stopping Nicholas from giving her what she had wanted so much. Of leaving a void that cried out for him.

'We haven't discussed actual plans for the wedding.' His words cut across her meandering thoughts. 'I'm reliably informed that there are hundreds of things that have to be taken care of. How do you want to go about this? Would you like to hire a wedding planner? Or handle the organising together, just you and I?'

Her head whipped around. Her gaze clashed with his. It was so easy to forget what had started all this. But she couldn't afford to forget. Not for a moment. Wedding plans? No, no, no. Quiet ceremony. Small. Easy to back out of.

'The wedding plans. Right.' She tried to pull herself together, to at least sound half-coherent. She gulped down a breath. 'Since we're keeping it small and intimate—' the word choked her to a stop, and she had to take a deep breath before she went on '—I want you to leave it all to me.'

It was the only possible way she could maintain control of the plans. Or rather keep from making any.

She gave an emphatic nod, and hoped she looked more confident and assured than she felt. 'I'm sure you'll be surprised by the results.'

'You want to totally surprise me, then? I won't be involved at all?' A mask slid over his face, blocking out his thoughts. One brow quirked in polite enquiry.

He wanted to be involved. Claire was positive of it. The man claimed to be made of concrete, but he wasn't. He did have feelings, just like everyone else. He just refused to let himself show them. Did he have any idea how much richer his life would be if he embraced his emotions rather than stuffing them into a box and sitting on the lid?

Oh, right, Claire. And you should encourage him to bring out those emotions, to expose them and explore them. So he can be really hurt at the end of this.

She hadn't meant that at all. Had got carried away with her thoughts for a moment, that was all. With her own foolish wish that they could grow close emotionally. It was happening to her more and more.

Focus on the conversation.

The wedding. Right. Oh, he would be surprised, all right.

She nodded—she hoped not desperately. 'Um, yes. I want to surprise you.'

'If that will please you.' He still seemed disappointed. 'I'll organise a transfer to your bank account, and you can just go for it, okay?'

Money she couldn't afford to spend. Would have to pay back if she did.

'I'm—uh—I've been living frugally, as I mentioned when you first visited my apartment. I have savings in the bank. You won't need to advance me anything. Certainly not soon, anyway.'

Because I won't be investing anything in our wedding plans. Because—well, because there won't be a wedding.

'How about if I let you know if I need a cash boost?' she suggested. 'That might be best.'

'Provided you make sure you do so.' He toasted her with his bottle of apple cider. 'Whatever makes you happy, Claire, makes me happy. I hope you'll remember that.'

The day went rather dim at that point. Oh, the sun kept shining, the sea stayed as sparkling and blue. But a shadow moved over Claire's heart and stayed there, and she just couldn't shake it off.

To cover her unease, she tried extra hard to be bubbly and happy, and asked to see and do everything she had read about in the brochure in their cabin earlier.

Nicholas did his best to accommodate her, just like a loving spouse would. As if that thought helped her any.

The rest of the afternoon passed in a blur, until at last they went to dinner—where at least she could share his company with others.

'You dance as gracefully as you do everything else.' His compliment brushed across the sensitive skin behind her ear, a forcible reminder that she was in trouble again. Already.

She wanted her boss. Physically, intimately. But she wanted more. A place in his heart. Fool that she was.

Being in Nicholas's arms did make a fool of her. When he held her reality and forbidden dreams mingled, blended until she couldn't distinguish one from the other.

She shivered and told herself *not* to melt into him. But it was too late. She was already melted. Melted, and overheated, and devastated by this man. And by her guilt over deceiving him.

'If I dance well, so do you.' She met his gaze, then regretted it when she noted the slow, burning intensity in his eyes. They were only just past the appetisers, still waiting on the main course. How on earth would she survive until dessert? Even if he only wanted her body, she didn't know if she could resist him. 'But, ah, perhaps we should rejoin the others?'

He gave a significant glance to the surrounding dancers. 'I doubt we'll be missed. Half of them are out here, and the other half seem to have migrated to the bar.'

'Oh.' She fell silent, and hoped the number would end before she gave in and simply laid her head to rest against his chest, where she wanted it most to be.

After that it seemed a good idea to fortify herself for the remaining ordeal of the evening. She helped herself to some of the island specialty fruit punch, and thought the less than subtle after-kick was just what she needed to bolster her courage.

'You've had a couple too many drinks, I think.'

Nicholas's observation cut right across what Claire knew was a *very* amusing anecdote.

It was late. Very late. A half-dozen fruit punches late. Everyone else seemed to have deserted them, leaving them alone at the long cloth-covered table.

'I was telling you a story, Nich—o—las. In case you hadn't noticed.' She enunciated each syllable of his name with great care, then frowned at him. 'Now you've rudely interrupted me, and I can't remember the rest of my tale.'

'Let's go back to the cabin.' His suggestion was accompanied by a wry smile. 'You can tell me the rest then, if you like.'

'Oh, well, I suppose that might be okay.' In the foggy recesses of her mind, something suggested that being alone with Nicholas wasn't supposed to be a good idea, but she couldn't quite think why. 'I'm yours to comm—comm—To tell what to do.'

'Right.'

Nicholas helped Claire out of the restaurant. And she needed quite a bit of help.

Outside, she stopped, a startled expression on her face. 'I'm three-parts sozzled, aren't I?'

'Yep.' He caught her arm as she stumbled again. 'You are that.'

'I didn't think the punch was that strong.' She pressed her lips to his ear to impart her secrets. 'It was for courage, you know.'

A shudder of response moved through him. Vulner-able like this, she made him want to protect her. To keep her close to his heart where nothing could harm her.

Damn, she had him twisted into knots. Inside, outside, sideways. He did his best to ignore the feelings. 'Yes, I know. Why don't you stop talking until we get back to the cabin?'

'I could, but I don't know if I'm going to make it to the cabin. I'm very wobbly.'

Her last words emerged in an endearing blur. He turned to smile at her, and caught her just in time as her legs crumpled under her.

'Home we go, little one.' He swept her into his arms, where she lay boneless and trusting against his chest. Exactly what he *didn't* need to feed the protective surges plaguing him. 'You've had about enough of life for today, I suspect.'

'Oh, no.' She shook her head, then wound her arms around his neck and pressed a kiss against the skin there. 'I'm okay. In fact....' She paused and pressed closer, lowered her voice. 'I really want you. I think it would be a good idea—no, a *great* idea, for you to make love to me, Nicholas. Please. In the cabin, not in the sea. Where nobody will see.' She giggled. 'Hear that? I rhymed.'

She might have been laughing, but her hands had risen to stroke the sides of his neck, offering both invitation and promise. And Nicholas wanted to take her. To possess her. As if in some way that would give him the right to protect her from the world as well.

There had always been secrets in Claire's eyes. No-go zones that Nicholas had wanted to break through. He wanted to get past those zones more than ever now, despite his belief that emotional involvement was a huge mistake.

It was. His own confusion right now was testimony to that.

They arrived at the cabin at that moment. Nicholas put off answering her until he had her safely inside. Although he wasn't sure if the word *safely* could be applied to any aspect of this situation.

'You think that would be a good idea, do you? Us making love where nobody can see?' His body was responding to holding her, to having her so close and so willing. But he couldn't take her. Not when she wasn't in control of herself. Not when *he* wasn't in control of *himself.*

He strode through to her room and lowered her onto the bed. 'Why don't you rest on that idea for a minute?'

'Don't need to rest. I'm quite wide awake, I promise you.' She clutched his shoulders. 'Don't go, Nicholas Monroe.' A giggle shot out of her mouth. 'I rhymed again.'

'Yes, I noticed that.' He also noticed how adorable she was. Adorable and completely at his mercy, damn it all.

'Stay with me, Nicholas.' She sighed and shifted voluptuously on the bedcovers. 'I know you want to.'

'That's true. I want to.' He pressed a deep kiss onto her mouth, one kiss only. He let himself savour her, warm and willing, for just a little bit. Then he took her arms from about him, tucked them close to her body, and rolled her onto her side. 'Go to sleep, Claire.'

'I don't want….' Her words drifted off and, although it clearly hadn't been her intention to do so, so did she.

Nicholas closed the door on her and left the cabin, in the hope that a few hours roaming the beach might cool him off. He really wasn't in the mood for a second sleepless night, but he had a feeling he was going to get one anyway.

CHAPTER SEVEN

'YOU'RE back early.' Nicholas spoke in surprise as he stepped out of his office space and into Claire's.

A slight frown marked his face, and Claire tried to smile. 'I guess I am a little early, but it's no use just taking up time for the sake of it.'

Two weeks had passed since Nicholas had proposed. Eleven days and somewhere around twelve hours had passed since Claire had drunk too much and made a fool of herself on the island.

Such a small amount of time, really, in the scheme of things, and yet it felt as though so much had happened. Burying herself in office work hadn't really alleviated any of her confusion or concern. On the surface she tried to maintain their professional relationship, but the control was only skin-deep. The feelings were

131

all still there, bubbling, frothing, threatening to flood over at the first provocation.

Nicholas seemed distracted, too. More reserved than usual. Sometimes, when their gazes clashed unexpectedly, his would soften. But invariably, afterwards, he would revert to keeping his distance.

It had been like that ever since they'd returned to Sydney from Brandmeire. At first she'd thought he was disgusted by her behaviour that night, but later she'd realised that, although she *had* made a fool of herself, they had both been a bit out of control that weekend.

Nicholas had simply decided, the same as she had, that he needed to take a step back. To get a bit of distance, a bit more control over himself and the situation. All the heat was still there in him too, but it was banked. He was being careful.

They'd been out half a dozen times. Dinner. The theatre. Nicholas had even managed to get prime seats at the Sydney Cricket Ground for a match between Australia and the West Indies one Saturday, and they'd spent hours with their noses slathered in green and yellow sunblock, cheering the home team along.

Go the Baggy Greens, Claire thought, and stifled a sigh. It hadn't been an easy two weeks. The one thing Nicholas *had* done was push for her to get wedding plans in motion. She hated the deceit of letting him think she was preparing when in fact she wasn't, but at least time was slowly passing. If Nicholas continued his withholding tactics, they just might make it through this whole thing after all.

Although it might not feel like it right now, that would actually be something to rejoice about.

She forced herself to meet his gaze. 'I've got things well in hand in relation to the wedding, Nicholas. Really.'

More deceit. She hated this. He had picked her because he appreciated her honesty. What a laugh that was turning out to be.

'If it's all the same to you—' she crossed her fingers behind her back '—I'd rather not take any more time off work for that reason.'

She couldn't hide out in coffee shops for ever, while she avoided making plans. Even with the generous lunch allowance Nicholas had given her, she couldn't go on eating cheesecake. Eventually even she would get sick of it. Or get fat on it. One or the other.

'It was generous of you to arrange time away from work for me, but it's not necessary.'

'Okay. I admit I pushed you into it without giving you a whole lot of choice.' He held up his hands. 'In my defence, I hadn't realised it would be so hard to leave everything to someone else—even if that someone is you. I'm accustomed to being in control, I suppose. It doesn't seem right not to know what's going on.'

'This isn't something I can give you control over.' At least not without revealing she hadn't done a blessed thing towards this so-called marriage merger. 'For that matter, you won't be getting control over me, either. Marriage is a joining, not a takeover.'

And listen to *her*, talking as though the wedding would actually take place. Sometimes even *she* didn't understand herself.

'That's not the point, though,' she hurried to say. 'I know you were only trying to help, and I appreciate the thought. Just perhaps not the execution of it.'

'I'm off the hook, then?' The question was teasing, assured. He was more relaxed today, somehow, which immediately raised her own tension.

She sighed. It seemed every time she took a breath something else happened. Like Nicholas trying to hide how much he wanted to stick his oar into the wedding plans. Sometimes he seemed almost vulnerable about it. And she still wanted, every time she looked at him, to jump on him and kiss him until her head blew off.

Not to mention make a home with him, make a family with him, and just generally make a happy-for-ever-after with him. That didn't help, either.

'Well.' Nicholas rubbed his hands together. 'I have good news for you, actually.'

'What's the news?' Something good would make a nice change. She searched her mind, but couldn't think of much. 'Closure on the

Campbell work? Last time I spoke with John Greaves he didn't have a lot to say about it.'

In fact, Greaves had been evasive and abrupt. But in Claire's experience that was typical. Ever since she'd walked in on him doing a deal with a bookmaker, John Greaves had made his dislike of her apparent.

The man shouldn't have been handling his personal business during office hours, but who was Claire to point fingers? For all she knew it might have been the only time it had happened, and everybody did stuff like that now and then.

'Think *personal*.' Nicholas shook his head. 'It's something to do with our wedding. Something you were waiting for. If I'd realised you'd be back early, you could have delivered the news yourself.'

No, *no*! There was only one piece of news she had insisted on delivering in person. A sense of dread washed over her—but it *couldn't* be about her sister. Sophie wasn't due back for ages yet. Her sister *had* to be safely out of the country still. Why on earth wouldn't she be?

'Your sister called in.' Nicholas confirmed the worst. 'It seems she and the Senator changed their plans and came back early.'

'I'd say *very early*. But why?'

'Sophie mentioned the holiday hadn't proved to be particularly relaxing after all, and that Tom had decided to do his canvassing from his home office.' He shrugged. 'Maybe they had a bit of a spat, or something. I didn't ask for details.'

A disagreement wouldn't surprise Claire. Sophie could be annoying, and although Tom was usually patient with her, maybe the shine had begun to wear off now that they'd been married a while.

The proverbial falling out of love, huh? Nicholas would feel vindicated, if he were the gloating kind.

Claire would have to make sure she caught up with Sophie. If there were problems, she wanted to encourage Sophie to do her best to fix them.

'Oh, well. It's nice that Sophie's back in the country.'

She tried to look pleased, when in fact her sister's return was the last thing she wanted right now. The ramifications didn't bear thinking about, and from Nicholas's pleased-with-himself expression...

It hit Claire just exactly what it really did mean.

'You told her.' She couldn't hide her dismay.

'When she realised you weren't here, she wasn't inclined to wait around.' His mouth took on a hard-edged look. 'I didn't want to miss the opportunity.'

Okay, This doesn't have to be a disaster. Telling Sophie we intend to get married doesn't have to alter anything. We're on a plan. The wedding isn't due to take place for another three and a half months. I'll just tell her it's going to be low-key, not to expect anything to be happening beforehand, and sort the rest out later.

Nicholas had overstepped his bounds, though. If only he had kept quiet Claire might still have thought of some way to avoid telling her sister at all.

'I wanted to be the one to tell Sophie the news.' *I never wanted to tell her a thing about you and me. I wanted it all to be over before Sophie got wind of it.* 'You don't know Sophie, Nicholas. You couldn't have had any idea how she might—'

'React to the news?' Challenge filled his tone. 'How close are you to your sister, Claire? I've noticed the couple of times she's called into the office there seemed to be an air of constraint between the two of you.'

Yes, because I'm paying off her blackmailer. A man who seems far too on edge for my comfort. And half the time I wonder if Sophie could care less, let alone give a damn about the financial sacrifices I'm making.

Sophie was her only sibling, but that didn't make her perfect. Only loved. At times, Claire's own ambivalence towards her sister caused her as much grief as Sophie herself did.

'She's my sister.' She folded her arms around her middle, then forced herself to uncross them. Blowed if she would allow herself to look defensive about this. 'You're in the wrong here, Nicholas. It was *my* job to tell

Sophie, and I resent that you took the opportunity away from me.'

'Even if it meant ensuring the Senator's wife behaves herself about the issue?'

At the startled widening of her eyes, he smiled. 'Oh, yes. It seems Mrs Senator thought it would be a grand idea to splash our wedding plans about in the media. With her as the delivering mouthpiece, of course.'

Claire stifled a groan. Why did things have to be so complicated? So unmanageable? So utterly worrying in so many different ways? She felt as though a trap was closing its jaws around her. If she didn't do something drastic, and quickly, this situation was going to end in disaster. She could feel it.

As if it hadn't reached that point already.

Nicholas strolled to her desk and seated himself casually on the corner of it. 'I think Sophie and I understood each other in the end. She's been given the happy tidings, and she is aware that those tidings are ours alone to share with the wider public. It will *have* to hit the news. Monroe's is too well-known for that to be avoided. But we can at least control the how and when of it.'

Panic threatened to overwhelm Claire. Things were moving too fast. In fact, they weren't supposed to be moving at all. There weren't supposed to be any changes, any hidden alterations to her plan. She felt as though what little amount of control she had was being ripped from her grasp.

'Yes, well—I would have liked to speak to her, myself.' She dropped into her chair, then got up again when she realised it put her too close to him. At this point bringing physical longing into the equation was the last thing she needed to add to her load. 'There are a couple of matters I wanted to discuss with her.'

There weren't really, but it was the principle of the thing.

'You'll get plenty of time to see her.' Nicholas swung one leg back and forth. His navy socks had tiny red diamond shapes dotted over them.

She stared at them, and wondered how on earth a man could have sexy ankles, and how a woman could tell even when he had on a pair of socks like that. But she could.

Then his words sank in, and she narrowed her gaze on his face. 'What do you mean?'

'Sophie and the Senator have business here in Sydney.' He smiled and got to his feet. 'It seems they'll be around until the weekend.'

'Oh, well, that's nice.' She took a step back. It wasn't retreat. She just wanted to put her bag away. With a quick movement she picked it up, stuffed it into the bottom drawer of the desk, then straightened warily.

Nicholas had the look of a prowling beast about him. The very air around them shrieked of that latent strength.

Claire didn't like it. 'I suppose I'll look out for Sophie, then. Did she leave the name of their hotel?'

'They're at the Rorriton.' He paced forward again, trapping her between the desk and her chair. 'Don't you think it's a good thing, Claire? That your sister is here in town and has a free weekend coming right up?'

'Uh, I guess so.' How did he expect her to think at all when he looked at her as though he wanted to devour her in a number of delectable, juicy bites?

'We're going to take advantage of their presence.' He leaned forward to place a hot kiss against the nape of her neck.

It was the first time he had done something so intimate at work, and it seemed all the more potent for that fact.

His breath teased her skin into such sensitivity that she froze to the spot. 'Why wait longer when we both know we want each other? We're ready for this.'

'What are you saying?' Somehow her hands had found their way to the column of his throat, and her fingers began to stroke. He was strong, full of vitality and leashed power. Her fingers recognised all these things, and wanted to help themselves to more. Claire drifted in a semi-blissful state, her mind releasing any desire to remain in tune with the conversation.

Her feelings were telling her to go with this. To enjoy touching him. And for once she was going to simply follow that leading.

'While your sister is here we're going to get married...' He half closed his eyes. His hands clenched on her shoulders in response to her touch. 'That's what I'm saying.'

'Oh, right...'

She continued to stroke, absorbed in the movement of muscle beneath his skin, until his words hit her. Her brain wrenched suddenly back into normal function mode. She reared back.

This wasn't just an unexpected bump in her plans. It was an outright eruption.

'What? We can't. We agreed to wait *four months*. We've picked a date. And there's so much to get done before we can possibly marry.'

You're threatening the escape clause in my contract, here.

'We did, and we have, and there is.' He inclined his head and took advantage of the movement to brush his mouth across hers, in an erotic byplay that made the blood roar through her veins. 'But I know you, Claire, and that organised mind of yours. I'll bet you have everything in good shape already. I'm sure we can sort out the license in time. If you need help to hurry things along, I'll do whatever you need. I promise.'

'No.' She shook her head. No way could she allow him to press her into getting married this weekend. 'I don't have things in good enough shape to cope with a wedding in two days' time. It would be unfair of you to ask that of me.'

When he didn't seem convinced, she pressed on, bringing out all the weapons she could think of. 'You let me have the task of organising the wedding, I believe, because you felt I would get enjoyment out of it. If we marry this weekend that enjoyment won't be possible for me. It'll be a rushed, hole-and-corner affair. Is that what you really want?'

'No. And if you'd been planning something enormous I'd understand your concerns.' The look he gave her suggested he believed he had her over a barrel. 'But you opted for a small, quiet wedding. That's not something that can't come together faster than we originally thought it would have to.'

'Sophie and Tom would make themselves available to attend our marriage at any time.'

Her sense of desperation edged up another notch. 'If you insist on bringing it forward, at least let's go for a more manageable timeframe.'

He folded his arms across his chest and lifted his chin. *Not* an agreeable stance. 'Like…?'

'Like two months from now.' She would have to work out a way to pay Sophie's old boss off two weeks earlier, but…

'That far away, we might as well wait until the original date we set.'

'Exactly.' She pounced, determined to pin him to that now that he had brought it up.

But Nicholas just shook his head. 'Is it pre-wedding jitters? You don't have to be afraid about this. I promise you, we're going to be good together.'

'I'd still like to have the wedding at least two months from now.' If she sounded truculent, it was because she was worried.

'I can't agree.'

She resisted the urge to start an agitated pacing of the office. 'One month, then.' How she would manage her last payment on that timeframe she simply didn't know. But she would try.

'Sorry.' He shook his head, his hazel eyes sharp and focussed on her face. 'No can do.'

'You're not going to give an inch about this, are you? Even though you've put me in a really awkward position?'

'When you think it over, you'll realise it'll be for the best.' One of his shoulders dipped and a corner of his mouth kicked up. 'Look at us. We've been skirting each other in this office since we got back from the island. Both of us have been holding back to try and keep things smooth. This way the waiting ends. We get together, get adjusted, and our work environment settles down again. We'll both be better off for it.'

Oh, it was all very clever and rational. *What am I going to do?* For a moment she thought she might hyperventilate. And the sad thing was, the thought of going off into an oblivious state held a lot of appeal.

'Easy!' Nicholas's arms tightened around her. 'You look as though you're about to fall over.'

'Lunch.' She pulled an excuse from the harried recesses of her mind. 'I missed out on eating.' *Except for that huge piece of cheesecake, and the coffee, and the little round chocolate thingy they stuck on top of the whipped cream, and the whipped cream itself. Boy, did she have depression, or what?* 'I was so busy.' *Avoiding making any wedding plans.*

'You're not to go without lunch again.'

Nicholas's demand somehow brought her back to reality. It was so bossy, so caring, even if couched with sternness. At the thought of this masculine care, even though he refused to believe it was part of his make-up, she almost cracked all over again.

He gave her shoulders a slight shake. 'Do you hear me?' Then he paused, searched her face. 'Tell me you're not dieting so you can fit into some stupidly tiny dress.'

More concern. So devious in its effect on her. She softened to mush—and mush was not a state to be in to extract herself from this situation. 'I'm not dieting to try and be something I'm not.' She touched his face, unable to resist.

'Then I expect to see you eating something you've ordered up from the coffee shop in the next ten minutes.' He released her and stepped back. 'Once you've got some food in your stomach, we'll discuss these upgraded wedding plans.' He rubbed his hands together. 'We only have a couple of days, so we need to move on it.'

'I want to talk to Sophie.' She needed to get a plan together. One that would enable her to avoid marrying this man two days from now. 'I think I'd better have the rest of that long lunch hour after all.'

'All right.' His expression softened.

He probably thought he had won, she decided uncharitably.

'Go.' He waved her away from her workstation. 'See your sister. Give yourself enough space to embrace the idea of bringing this wedding forward. When you do, you'll be glad about it. I promise.'

'You think so?'

They *couldn't* get married. That was all there was to it. He would want to share a bed, but not his heart. To blend their lives, but not open to her the thoughts and dreams that shaped him.

And she? She would be dying inside from all the deceit, the evasion. Most of all she would be dying from what Nicholas refused to give her of himself. She couldn't live like that, in a loveless void.

'Congrats on the upcoming nuptials.' Sophie had been sprawled on a king-size bed when Claire had entered the suite of rooms at the Rorriton Hotel. Now she got up. 'I was surprised when Nicholas told me the news.'

She looked pale and drawn, but she took a bag from the corner of the room and handed it to Claire. 'This is for you, from France. A very exclusive brand, and it cost me the earth, but the moment I saw it I knew it would suit you.'

'Oh, Sophie.' Claire drew the silk purse out of its layers of tissue paper and shook her head. It was a generous thought. But Sophie's extravagant ways were the reason they were in this mess. She tried to stem the rising tide of hysteria, but was only partially successful.

Sophie leaned forward, hope clear on her face. 'Do you like it?'

Claire looked at her feckless, generous, frustrating little sister, and firmed a mouth that suddenly wanted to tremble. She laid the purse down on the bed and said something she couldn't ever remember saying to Sophie before. 'I'm in trouble.'

Sophie started to laugh, then stopped. 'You're serious?'

'Yes.' Claire started to pace the plush carpeted room, her fists clenching and unclenching. 'Two weeks ago, out of the blue, my boss offered me a choice. An emotionless marriage or a return to the clerical pool.' The words tumbled over each other in a babbling rush that Claire couldn't slow. 'When I realised he was serious I had to say I'd marry him, to buy time to save up the final blackmail payment. It was for *you*, Sophie. I had to do it for you. I told him we had to keep the engagement secret, and wait four months to get married—until you came back from your trip. I planned to make the payment, then back out of the engagement.'

Sophie gasped. 'I had no idea. I thought the two of you must be in love.'

'Love?' A laugh shot out of Claire's mouth, and another, before she could clamp down on them. 'No. It's not love. But Nicholas is determined to get married straight away now that you're back and he's told you the news. He's adamant that the wedding will go through this Saturday.'

'Oh, my God, Claire.' Sophie's eyes widened into saucers. 'What are you going to do?'

Claire pressed a fist against her mouth. 'Not me, Soph. *You.*' Claire had given up a lot of things to try and help Sophie. Now it was her sister's turn. 'You have to get the rest of the blackmail money. Right now. So Haynes can be paid and the wedding can be called off.'

The thought of Nicholas's reaction when she did that made her sick to her stomach. And the idea of never seeing him again hurt far more.

'I'll hand in my resignation. Find another job. Start over.' She tried to sound as though she were looking on the bright side. 'At least it'll be finished.'

'Oh, Claire.' Sophie crumpled onto the bed in a guilty heap. 'I've done this to you. I was the one who got into trouble, then ran to you to fix it. This is all my fault. I'm sorry.'

Claire searched Sophie's face and realised she *was* genuinely remorseful. When Sophie rose, arms outstretched, Claire went into the hug. It was the first they'd shared in a long time, and she could feel Sophie shaking before they parted.

She told Sophie how much money she still needed to make the last payment.

Sophie gasped. 'I'll give you every cent of my allowance,' she promised earnestly, 'but I only have eight hundred dollars.'

Eight hundred dollars? That was all? Claire shook her head. 'You'll have to tell Tom the truth. Get him to give you the rest. I realise you didn't want him to know, but this is no time to hold back. I always believed you should have told him, anyway.'

At that Sophie fell apart completely, sobbing as though her heart would break. 'I can't,' she whispered. 'Oh, Claire. I've made such a mess of things.'

Claire's heart skipped a beat. 'What do you mean?'

'Tom and I...' Sophie took a tissue from the box beside the bed and wiped her eyes. 'Our marriage has been strained lately. We've been trying for a baby for months and months and months. And now I'm finally pregnant.' She drew a shuddery breath. 'But when we went overseas I felt so miserable with it that I guess I consoled myself a bit too much in the shops. Tom got angry about the amount of money I was spending...'

'Oh, Sophie, no.' Claire didn't even want to hear this.

'Yes. That's what happened.' Sophie's head bobbed up and down. 'Tom said that from now on he's going to be watching every cent until I prove I can be responsible. That brought out other things, and we ended up fighting so badly that he called the trip off.'

She gave a sobbing hiccup. 'We only stopped here in Sydney so he could do some business, and I've barely seen him since we arrived.' When she looked up, her eyes were red from weeping. 'I hadn't realised how much

I love him. How much I want to have this baby with him and be happy together.'

'I can understand that, Sophie, but—'

'If I tell him about the blackmail now, or ask for more money, he'll leave me. I know it.' Sophie grabbed another tissue and started shredding it with her fingers in agitated, jerky motions. 'I know I have to tell him the truth eventually. I can see now that it was wrong to deceive him. But I have to have a chance to prove myself to him first.'

'But you were my only chance.' Claire's world was crumbling, but she couldn't seem to comprehend the enormity of it. She knew only that she had run out of options.

Sophie sat up straighter. 'I could try to sell some of my jewellery and dresses. Or get a job and give you some of that money.'

For a moment hope surged in Claire. Then she shook her head. 'Tom would notice if things were missing. And if you got a job he'd want to know where all the money was going. But thank you for offering.'

Her sister *was* redeemable. At least Claire knew that much. And she'd need every bit of strength she could draw from it to go through with the wedding.

Torment rolled through her as she acknowledged how thoroughly she was trapped. Although their circumstances were different, Claire couldn't tell Nicholas the truth any more than Sophie could tell Tom.

Claire had to go through with the wedding. Had to go on deceiving Nicholas until she had paid the blackmailer off. And then she had to walk away.

She was hopeful for her sister's future. But for herself she had never felt so helpless, confused and heartsore. The only thing left to do to control the damage, to protect her heart from even more pain, was to make certain she and Nicholas never made love.

CHAPTER EIGHT

SATURDAY came quickly. Before Claire knew it, she was standing in the chapel, in front of God and everybody, eaten up with guilt, about to begin a marriage that must never be consummated.

Her final gift to Nicholas would be a quick annulment. It wasn't the kind of thought that brides usually had as they stood before the altar.

How ironic that his hasty plans had come together so wonderfully, right down to the beauty of this old building. The chapel had a timeless elegance that showed in every bold architectural stroke.

Garbed in its wedding finery, it shone even more. The polished wood pews and stained-glass windows formed a perfect backdrop for the branches of apple blossom and the dozens upon dozens of tapered white candles that gave out a soft welcoming glow.

With the help of a very efficient, forgiving, and most of all *discreet* wedding planner, Claire had managed quite a presentable effort. On the surface, things looked fine. She even looked fine herself, in an off-the-shoulder white satin sheath gown overlaid with French lace.

Their respective family and close friends filled a few rows of the church behind them, smiling benevolently while cameras flashed. But Claire was about to exchange marriage vows with the boss. The thought was terrifying.

Her gaze strayed to where Nicholas stood at her side before the Reverend. Each day deepened her love for him, and that was another reason she had to keep this marriage platonic.

If she wanted to survive at all, she couldn't afford to tumble any further, and she knew if they made love any defences she still had in place would collapse. Then she wouldn't only tumble, she would plunge headlong and lose herself for all time.

How she wished she could tell Nicholas everything. But he would despise her, and then send her away, and none of her problems would be solved. She was trapped in her own web of deceit, and it was going to get worse before it got better.

She couldn't face the thought of the heartbreak ahead. And, on top of that, she had to fight the attraction that seemed to want to consume them both at every turn.

Nicholas had made no secret of his desire for her. Claire wanted him, too. Any time they were in a room together she sizzled with awareness of him. With need and desire and want. And it was all for him. Only for him.

And that only scratched the surface of her feelings. He claimed to be uninterested in the emotions that bound couples together, but for a man with such a cynical view he could be incredibly thoughtful. That only made her care for him more.

Of course that was when he wasn't forcing her into instant marriage.

The truth was, she wanted all this to be real. She wanted it to be love that shone from Nicholas's deep hazel eyes, not simply self-satisfaction. It *was* only satisfaction, wasn't it?

Yet when she gazed back at him she saw emotion of *some* kind.

No. He can't have feelings about this. It's just desire. Lust.

Because if it wasn't, then she was not only in for the heartbreak of a lifetime, but she was going to hurt him unbearably, too.

'Please join your right hands,' the Reverend intoned, and they did so.

Claire's heart lurched at even that contact, and her gaze flew to Nicholas's, and caught there.

'Do you, Claire Maree...?' the Reverend began.

The pounding of her pulse in her ears drowned out the rest. When the Reverend's lips stopped moving, she closed her eyes, unable to look at Nicholas as she answered the question that should have bound them for a lifetime. 'I do.' *And I wish with all my heart it could all be true.*

'And do you, Nicholas Anthony...?'

Nicholas's grip on her hand tightened. 'I do.'

His answer rang with conviction and satisfaction, and Claire's heart ached so much she thought it might actually break. Nicholas looked at her, and sensual fire arced between them, surrounded them.

She ached to throw herself forward and soak him in through the very pores of her being. To fill her soul with his soul and keep him there for ever.

The Reverend cleared his throat. 'You may kiss the bride.'

Nicholas didn't waste any time. He swept her into his arms and gave her the kiss she had fantasised about since she'd come to his side at the beginning of the service. A kiss of heat and possession and promise, of sweetness and strength. His hands crushed the lace of her gown, and reality, and his searing kiss, pronounced them man and wife.

She was Mrs Nicholas Monroe. Her mouth trembled beneath his. It took all her composure not to break down as he released her lips and tucked her hand into the crook of his elbow, just as he had that day they walked the city streets to meet the Forresters for lunch.

Perhaps it was just as well that they had to face the well-wishers at that moment, or Claire might have given way to the urge to bawl like a baby. *Or run.* Or maybe bawl like a baby *and* run.

I can get through this. I can.

Then there would be afterwards to get through. Tonight. Next week. And all the days until she paid off Sophie's blackmailer. She couldn't bear to think about that now.

'Congratulations.'

'So happy for you.'

'Come, let me kiss you, darling. She's so beautiful. I know you'll be wonderfully, wonderfully happy.'

This from Nicholas's mother, floating in yards of pale green silk, the jewels on her fingers worth a small fortune by themselves.

Nicholas leaned forward to receive his mother's kiss on the cheek. He seemed comfortable enough with her, any past demons at rest. Claire didn't feel so charitable.

Claire might never have known the truth of Nicholas's mother's desertion of them years ago if she hadn't shared a taxi ride with his youngest brother yesterday, at the rushed rehearsal.

She glanced at Colin now, and wondered how three brothers could be so different. Colin had told her about his parents, whereas her own fiancé had been so reserved when it came to his personal life. And Damon was different again, aloof in a way even Nicholas didn't achieve.

And their father... She turned as he approached, received his kiss on her cheek with both guilt and respect.

'I know he finds it difficult to show his feelings, Claire, but don't ever give up on him. You're obviously the one who can help dig out his heart from under the rubble his mother and I caused.' The words were whispered before he stepped away from her.

Claire shook her head, denying it. Nicholas wouldn't give her his heart. He had it locked away in a place nobody would ever reach, and it was better that way. Better for him. When she left him he would be okay.

I'll pay back every cent this cost. Somehow. Even those cheesecake lunches.

As if that would make it all better. But it was all she had to offer as any form of compensation or apology.

Sophie came forward in a cloud of French perfume. She looked better today, and Tom stood at her back, his hand possessively on her shoulder. Claire hoped it would last.

Sophie leaned forward to whisper in Claire's ear. 'I'm praying that somehow you'll find a way to be happy. You deserve it.'

If only that could be so. Claire's eyes misted, but she gave Sophie a hug. 'I want you to know, whatever happens from here on in, I'm proud of you for trying to change.'

'I'm probably always going to be a spend-thrift,' Sophie admitted. 'And I doubt I'll ever settle to plain old domesticity. But I'm doing what I can.'

The photo session was a strain. Nicholas orchestrated the other players so firmly and smoothly Claire doubted they even knew they were being manoeuvred. The family got their ten minutes to share the fame, and were cheerfully ousted to the bar afterwards. Then Claire and Nicholas had to pose for the single shots, and she ached all over again.

To be in his arms, even with photographers looking on and ordering the poses, was sheer torture.

They gave a small, select section of the press five minutes to snap photos and ask questions—most of which Nicholas fielded without really telling them anything.

When it ended, they joined their guests in the function room of an exclusive club for a sumptuous buffet-style meal.

Claire took a few deep breaths to try to calm herself.

'Are you all right? You seem pensive.' Nicholas's dark head bent to hers.

Claire wanted to pull him the rest of the way, until their lips could meet and hold. Until she could lose herself in him, let herself have all that she wanted from him. If only there wouldn't be consequences.

'I don't think I like the press much.' It was an excuse for feelings that had plagued her all day, not just in the past ten minutes, but Nicholas let it go by—much to her relief.

'Now, if only my parents will leave each other alone,' he murmured, 'we might survive the rest of this.'

His words startled her. She hadn't expected him to confront the matter of his parents' relationship openly. But, then, they were married now. Maybe that made a difference to him. As in, he felt he could trust her now. Her eyes smarted.

'We've done what we can to keep everybody under control.' Her voice didn't reveal her emotion, thank goodness. They *had* done their best. By eliminating the formal eating arrangements they'd also done away with the speeches and some of the other conventions, which kept Nicholas's parents pretty much out of it.

Other traditions couldn't be so easily overlooked, however. Before she could prepare for it Claire was wrapped in Nicholas's arms, slowly circling the small dance floor in the steps of the bridal waltz.

'Today I've made you mine.' His words brushed against her ear, fluttering the curls that softened the upswept arrangement of her hair.

In those few words he branded her, claimed her, and left her aching. All at once.

How could she possibly keep this marriage platonic until the blackmailer was out of her and Sophie's lives? How could she deny Nicholas when she wanted him so much?

She took a sharp breath, but that was a mistake, too. The scent of apple blossom wafted between them. From the circlet surrounding her wrist, from the buttonhole in his charcoal-grey tuxedo. From the air around them.

It made her think of what they had done today, of the vows they had exchanged, and of how much she wanted them to belong together in reality.

'Mine for the rest of our lives, Claire.' Was he reading her mind? His eyes gazed down at her, fathomless, full of secrets and promises and desire. 'Are you happy?'

Could a person be happy and desperately sad all at the same time? If this were only real... If he loved her, rather than just wanted to possess her. If she could give herself to him without regret...

Oh, Lord. She didn't love him. Did she? As in wholly and completely? No going back? Forgoing an answer, both to him and to the questions in her head, she twined her arms around his neck and let her body melt into his.

Surely for just a few minutes she could have at least some of what she craved? Surely later would be time enough to step back, to get things under control again? How much harm could she come to in a crowded room, in full view of their wedding guests?

They would all expect this from the newly married couple, after all. 'I'm happy to be dancing with the most appealing, sophisticated, and utterly compelling man in the room. I know that much.'

Her words got more of a reaction than she'd bargained on. He tugged her closer and heat flared in his eyes.

'I want to get you alone,' he said. 'How soon can we ditch these people and leave?'

His growled words of desire sent a shiver through Claire. And a warning. It had been a mistake to press closer. To try to take something from him and think she could stop at just one small nibble, when what she wanted to do was devour him whole.

She took refuge in the practical, tipping her head up to smile at him as though her body wasn't humming with need for his. As though her heart wasn't turning back the comforter and inviting him to take his rest within.

'We may have managed to avoid any speeches, but this is still a wedding. There are one or two other matters to get through yet before we can leave.'

Things like separating to dance with their relatives—only Nicholas refused to let her go. His arms simply tightened about her as the waltz ended and other couples joined them on the floor for the following numbers.

After twenty minutes in his arms Claire's entire being buzzed with desire. Frustration filled her and left her aching. Just aching, heart, body, and soul, for this man who had become her husband. She hadn't consumed more than half a glass of champagne, yet she felt inebriated. Drunk on her need for Nicholas.

They cut the cake. A five tiered masterpiece of rich, brandy-soaked fruit encased in the softest, whitest frosting imaginable. When Nicholas placed a morsel of the treat upon her tongue, his fingers lingered to trace her lips. She closed her mouth over the food, and him, and her heart stuttered.

Her senses were wholly besieged by him. It was unbearable torture. But somehow she had to endure, and at the end hope her heart had survived the journey.

Shaking, quaking inside, she returned the favour, offering cake to him. And she didn't know whether to feel triumph or despair when heat stole into his cheekbones and he crushed her to him, his mouth coming down over hers in a kiss that tasted of brandied cake and his desire.

The cheering and whistling of their guests brought them apart. Nicholas took her hand in his and led her through the throng, stopping to chat to this one and that.

When it came time to toss the bouquet, Claire again broke with tradition. She walked to her sister and handed it to her. 'You're already married, but you're my only family. I want you to have this.'

Sophie smiled prettily while the other guests grinned their approval. Suddenly Nicholas swept Claire up into his arms and dropped her onto a nearby chair, where he proceeded to remove the garter from her thigh.

The whole thing happened in seconds, and his broad back shielded her from the view of the guests, but her shudders kept coming long after he released her to toss the article at one of his brothers. She was so eaten up with frustration and need she didn't even see which one received the garter.

'I need to change.' She tried to smile at Nicholas, but the smile was crooked. *I need to get out of here. To take a deep breath. To stop wanting you so badly that I ache all the way to the backs of my teeth.*

His dark gaze seared over her. 'If I didn't want to preserve that dress intact, I'd offer to help you. But I fear I'd end up ripping it, rather than having the patience to take it off you properly.'

Claire hurried away, turning down Sophie's offer to help her change. But when she was alone she regretted the solitude that gave her too much time to think.

As she removed the beautiful dress, guilt bombarded her again. A lot of money had been spent on this marriage. The news of their nuptials would be all over Australia by tomorrow. When she left Nicholas he would have to deal with the fallout.

And none of that took into account what might happen when they finally left this reception and found themselves alone.

She had done all this for her sister's sake—had made the best of two bad choices. At least Sophie was having a go now, but that didn't make the thought of the rest of this day any easier for Claire.

Dressed in her pale pink going-away dress, a shimmering concoction that swirled to mid-calf, she hovered, trying to build up the confidence to go back out there and face the remainder of the reception.

Into this dithering panic Nicholas strode, his black trousers and midnight-blue shirt testament to the fact that he, too, had changed clothes. His gaze flicked over her before he took her arm in a firm grip.

'I think you're finished here.' And, that simply, he swept her out of the room, out of the reception, and away.

Silence reigned as they drove towards his home. Claire doubted she could have spoken in any case, her nerves were so stretched. She glanced at him in the darkness. What was he thinking? What was going through his mind right now?

Sex. It's the night of your marriage and you haven't slept together before this. What do you think is going through his mind?

Which left Claire facing the same dilemma that had gnawed at her since Nicholas had calmly announced his intention to move the wedding forward. She had to convince him they couldn't consummate this marriage yet.

She was still rehearsing her speech on the subject when they arrived. As they approached the front door of the house, and Nicholas disabled the alarm, she opened her mouth to begin this all-important discussion.

No words came out, however. Just a startled squeak as Nicholas swept her into his arms and carried her over the threshold.

Oh, the heat of him. The sheer perfect male magnetism of him. Her arms had gone automatically around his neck, and being held this way felt so right. A homecoming for her heart as well as her senses. Against her will, her arms tightened, and that seemed to be all the encouragement he needed.

He kicked the door shut with a growl, lowered her, and fixed his mouth over hers in hot, demanding plunder. For a long, long moment she simply drowned. His lips tasted hers. Their tongues tangled and clashed.

She felt him trembling, and another piece of her was lost to him for all time. Then his hands seemed to be everywhere. Cupping her face, caressing her shoulders. Roving across her back, her hips, tugging her closer and ever closer, until not even a whisper would have fitted between them.

'Claire…Claire…' His voice scraped across her senses like fine-grade sandpaper. Wound around her heart and refused to let go. 'You take my breath away.'

She melted into him then—and who knew what would have happened if the sensation of cool air and hot hands against her bare back hadn't brought her to her senses? To the realisation that not only had Nicholas lowered the zipper on her dress, but she must have unbuttoned his shirt, too. For it now lay open, and her hands were pressed to hard, hot, man-chest.

'Ah!' She pulled her hands back as though burnt and stared at him, panting as she struggled to regain her control.

His hair was ruffled, his face tinged high on the cheekbones with the deep flush of desire. Before she lost the single shred of control she had managed to find, she broke out of his embrace and backed away.

He took a step forward, then stopped, eyes narrowed. 'What's going on, Claire?'

'I can't.' So much for her wonderful rehearsed speech on the subject of getting to know him better. Of having those many extra weeks of courtship that had been denied her by this hasty wedding.

As an argument for celibacy, it may not have been bulletproof, but it was better than this.

She flapped a hand, hating her incoherency. 'We can't do this.'

Again, that deep bass growl. Only this time it held a thread of annoyance. 'Can't do what? It seems to me we were doing just fine. Would you rather move up to the bedroom now? Is that the problem? If so, I'm happy to oblige. We'd have made our way there soon, anyway.'

'Would we?' She suspected they could as easily have ended up celebrating their nuptials right here in the entry hall. But that was hardly to the point, she supposed. 'It's not about location. I meant we can't make love.'

Finally. A complete sentence that was actually articulate. Maybe she would get there yet.

'Why not?' The question snapped out of him. 'Is this some sort of game?' Each short burst of words was colder than the last. His face was full of suspicion.

'It's no game. I just can't sleep with you, that's all.' She drew breath to explain her reasoning.

'You have your period?' His tone dismissed the potential problem before she could say anything at all.

Heat flooded into her face. 'No. It's not that.' She could have lied. Could have said she had her period and couldn't stand the thought of intimacy during that time. It wouldn't have been true—and what would it have bought her? A few days and one more untruth to add to all the rest?

She raised her chin and set her argument in motion at last. 'I need more time to get to know you. I already explained—'

'That was before we became man and wife.' He tipped back his head to glare at her. 'That was before today. Before you practically crawled inside me to get closer. There's no need to wait any longer, Claire. You know it. I know it. What's the real reason? What is it you want? What are you after? Money? Promises? Fancy gifts? What?'

Claire forgot her argument. Forgot everything but the hurt that sliced through her. 'I would *never* try to extort money out of you.' The words were low, harsh. 'I can't believe you would suggest such a thing.'

A muscle ticked in his jaw. His eyes were dark and fierce. Unyielding. 'What else am I supposed to assume? You have a strange way of showing your commitment to your new husband, you have to admit.'

'Stranger still that my husband would accuse me of such a money-grabbing interest in him.' A picture of the gold leaf jewellery flashed through her mind. Had he been buying her then, too?

All of a sudden her throat closed up. If she didn't escape, and quickly, she would break down. And she couldn't bear for him to see that.

'I'm tired.' Her glance moved to the stairs. 'I've had a gruelling forty-eight hours, preparing for a wedding that you insisted be moved forward by *months*. I'm going to bed. Alone. In one of the spare rooms.'

'*Claire.*' One lone word, growled in a warning tone.

His hands clenched and unclenched at his sides, but she didn't wait to see what he might say or do next.

Instead, she ran up the stairs, snagged one of her bags from the floor of the master bedroom, then hurried into another of the rooms and slammed the door behind her.

Only then did she allow the agony free rein. She threw herself onto the bed and let the tears flow. It might be a sham marriage from her perspective, anyway, but that didn't stop his words from hurting her.

CHAPTER NINE

CLAIRE woke to the scent of fresh coffee wafting in the air, and with a feeling of foreboding deep in the pit of her stomach. The previous night's debacle rushed back to fill her thoughts, and she pulled the pillow over her head with a low groan.

She had made such a mess of things. What must Nicholas think of her now? How could she face him after the way they had parted? This was much worse than her wanton behaviour on Brandmeire Island.

And there was so much more at stake now. Despite Nicholas's warnings, she was emotionally involved up to the eyeballs.

'Ignoring it won't make it go away,' she muttered into the pillow. 'You have two and a half months to get through before you can pay off the blackmailer and annul the marriage, and you can't spend all that time locked in this room. Sooner or later you have to face him.'

She lifted the pillow away. Actually, the house was incredibly quiet. Maybe he had made coffee and then gone out somewhere? She glanced at the clock on the bedside table.

Eight a.m. Sunday morning. Was Nicholas home? Or out? The wuss in her came to the surface and she uttered a whispered plea. 'Please let him be out.'

A sharp rap sounded on the closed door. She jumped in the bed, then froze, heart pounding. So much for that hope.

'Claire? Throw some clothes on and come out for breakfast. We need to talk.'

The effect of that gravelly voice on her nerve-endings was no less compelling than yesterday. Only now she had nervous anticipation to add to her list of other reactions to him.

Much as she wanted to lie there and pretend ignorance, she knew it would be a waste of time. She scrambled out of bed and headed for her bag. 'Give me a few minutes.'

He grunted something through the closed door, and then his footsteps receded and she heard muffled kitchen-type noises in the distance. The clatter of a pan against a stove-top, the rattle of ceramics. She dug through her bag and came up with a pair of white jeans and a pale blue T-shirt.

The rest of her possessions were stored in one of the other rooms here, awaiting her further instructions. Her old apartment was closed up, the keys handed over. When she left here she would be homeless, as well as jobless. Another problem she didn't want to think about.

Two minutes later she stood in the kitchen doorway and watched her husband flip perfect fluffy omelettes onto matching plates. He looked so domestic, and so utterly ravishing, with his dark hair mussed as though he had run his fingers through it a number of times.

A tight band closed around Claire's heart. A band of loss for the shared life with Nicholas that she wanted so much and couldn't have. These few weeks were all she would ever hold of him, and so far they didn't look to be starting out well.

When he turned to carry the food to the table, she pried herself away from the doorframe and stepped into the room.

'Good morning.' She searched his face for a clue to his frame of mind. He would be angry with her, of course. He had every right to be. But what else was he feeling? Had he allowed his emotions to get involved in this matter? Or was he holding back, as he had earlier claimed he always would? 'The, uh, the omelettes smell delicious.'

'Have a seat. They're best eaten hot.' He set the plates down on cork mats and turned to bring a coffee jug to the table, along with mugs, cream and sugar.

His movements were economical and sure. Claire's gaze fixed on his hands. She watched his deft movements with a hollow feeling inside. She wanted those hands on her, to soothe as well as to caress.

Last night's altercation had put paid to any chance of the soothing part happening, and she had to ensure the other didn't happen either. Even though it was for the best, she found little comfort in the thought.

When she'd taken her seat, Nicholas poured coffee for her and passed it. She added a dash of cream, and hoped he hadn't noticed the shaking of her hand.

'Do you feel better this morning?' His gaze on her was direct and determined. 'I don't think I've ever seen you lose your poise so completely.'

'I'm sorry.' She had spent half the night going over what had happened, and wishing she had at least handled it better. 'I know you're angry—'

'I was angry last night, I admit. It was my wedding night and I expected to spend it making love to my new wife. Not listening to her tossing and turning in a bed along the corridor from my own.'

He took a sip of coffee and set the mug down, then pinned her again with his glance.

'Whatever your problem is, Claire, I want it mended. We have a marriage to get on with. Either you tell me what the trouble is and we fix it together, or you tell me the problem is solved. Which is it to be?'

Claire hit back, stung by his animosity. 'You don't have a lot of patience, do you? And last night you accused me of trying to manipulate you.'

She hadn't meant to bring up the accusation. After all, she had done many things to him that she wasn't proud of—had thoroughly misled him from the beginning of this farcical relationship and continued to do so.

'Maybe you should forget I said that.'

'And maybe I shouldn't.' His grimace seemed to be directed inwardly before he lowered his gaze and dug a fork into his omelette. After a long moment of silence he spoke again. 'If you were too overwrought last night to make love, I would have simply held you, Claire. I'm not a monster.'

Claire wanted his arms around her right now, offering comfort, forgiveness, shelter. But if she took those things it would lead to making love. She stared at his face, more familiar to her now than her own, and ached for her losses.

'I can't get that close to you. It would—' She broke off, appalled that she had almost spilled the truth of it. That if she let him make love to her she would no longer be able to convince herself she wasn't *in love* with him.

'It's imperative that you *do* get that close to me.' Nicholas finished the last bite of food from his plate and set it aside. 'And you can prove your willingness by coming out with me this morning. As it happens, I've had a summons from the Forresters. It seems Jack is ready to get serious about this business deal at last. He wants to discuss it today.'

'That's great.' She tried to feed appropriate enthusiasm into her tone even as she wondered what right Jack Forrester thought he had to commandeer Nicholas's time the very day after his wedding.

Then again, the Forresters had been guests at the marriage and reception. Perhaps Nicholas had told them there was to be no honeymoon period?

'I hope something good comes out of the meeting. I'll be glad to come along to the office with you.'

His gaze challenged her. 'Actually, Jack and his wife have invited us to share a day on the ocean with them in their yacht. We leave straight after breakfast.'

Out of the question.

When she didn't immediately respond, he touched her hand where it rested on the table. 'It'll do us both good to get out.'

He was giving her a second chance. Trying to be nice about it. Claire couldn't respond in kind.

'I won't go.' The words were pulled from her. They were the last ones he would want to hear, and she knew it, but still her heart hammered with dread. She glanced at the grey sky. 'I don't think you should go, either.'

'Trying to manipulate me, Claire?'

'No. That's not what I meant.' She returned his stare miserably. 'You know I don't like the ocean.'

'You got past that.' His jaw squared. 'You'll come along today. I insist.'

'And I insist that I won't. This isn't even really about me going on a yacht with you. It's about us sleeping together, and I haven't changed my mind.' She hauled in a shaky breath. 'You owe me the right not to sleep with you until our original wedding date arrives.'

'That's stupid.'

'Whether you think so or not, it's how it's going to be.' He wouldn't force her, so she didn't see how he could argue the point any further.

For a long moment they stared each other down. Then, with a muttered oath, he got up and strode from the room. Moments later, the front door slammed behind him.

When the wind whipped the front door of the house from Nicholas's weary hands at midnight that night, crashing it against the inner wall as the storm continued to pelt rain down from all directions, Claire ran towards him with a cry.

'Are you all right? What happened to you? I've been worried sick.' Her face was pale, her eyes dilated with fear.

Nicholas looked at her anxious face. They had parted in anger. Something he had regretted soon after he left. Now her concern warmed him somewhere deep that had felt very cold. Any remaining traces of anger drained out of him, leaving him simply wanting to hold her. To be reconciled.

'It got pretty rough out there. Took us a while to get the yacht back into harbour.'

He raised a hand to brush his rain-soaked hair away from his face. It was still rough. He'd had a job getting home at all, but he didn't tell her that.

She looked at his arm, and paled even further. 'You're hurt.'

'It's nothing.' He glanced at the shallow gash that ran from elbow to wrist. 'Just a scratch.'

Her mouth worked for a moment, then she seemed to fill up with indignation. 'How dare you call it a scratch? How dare you be so irresponsible with your life? You could have been killed out there.'

'Hey.' He reached a hand towards her, then let it drop to his side. 'It wasn't that bad.'

'It *was* that bad.' Tears welled into her eyes and spilled over. 'I could have lost you.'

In that moment Nicholas saw two things very clearly. One, despite the fact that she refused to share his bed his wife cared about him. Enough to have worried herself crazy as the storm unleashed its fury all over Sydney. And two, *he* cared about *her*. More than he had realised could be possible.

Oh, not love. He rejected that thought. But he *cared*. Knowing she cared, too, released him somehow. He wanted to comfort her. To forget the past twenty-four hours and start again from here. He hoped that was possible.

'I'm sorry you were worried. I should have called when I got back to shore. I'm afraid I just didn't think you'd—'

He got no further, because Claire had flung herself into his arms and was squeezing the life out of him, arms tightly clenched around his middle, face pressed hard against his soaked shirt as lightning flashed through the windows and thunder clapped over their heads.

'Don't ever do that to me again.' She released her hold long enough to drum both fists against his chest before she locked him close again. 'I couldn't bear losing you, too.'

'You didn't lose me.' He lifted her chin with his hand and searched her face. 'I'm right here.

I'll always be here for you, Claire. For ever and ever.' He pressed his mouth to hers and tasted the salt of her tears, the tang of her fear.

Reassuring her was imperative. Nothing had ever mattered so much. Later he might pause to wonder at that thought. For now he tucked her closer and gentled her with his lips and his hands and the closeness of his body.

They kissed like that for long moments before she shuddered and eased her hold on him, then pulled back to look into his eyes. 'I want to tend to that cut on your arm. It shouldn't be left as it is.'

'All right.' If nurturing him helped her, he would go along with it. 'I should get out of these wet clothes, anyway.'

'Come upstairs.' She tugged on his uninjured arm. 'You're probably chilled through. You should have a hot shower, as well, to warm you up.'

'Holding you is all the added warmth I need.' When she looked askance at him, he shrugged. 'Feel my skin. Does it seem cold to you? You make me hot, Claire, whether you want to know about it or not.'

She blushed. Beautifully. Like a brand-new bride just realising her attraction. And mumbled something under her breath.

'What was that?' He climbed the stairs behind her, his gaze on the sway of her bottom in the white jeans, his heart inexplicably touched by her sweet reaction. 'I didn't hear you.'

Claire turned and caught him looking at her. She flushed afresh, and this time he could see desire in her, alongside an awareness of how she appealed to him.

When she spoke her mouth was soft, vulnerable. 'I said we'll just tend your arm, then. You can skip the shower part of it.'

The spacious bathroom seemed smaller with both of them in there, with Claire at his side, fussing over him. He sent her to get fresh clothes, and stripped down in her absence, rubbing his flesh and hair vigorously until he was completely dry. He had just tucked a towel around his waist when she stepped back into the room.

Her eyes widened, but she handed him the clothing and started to rummage through the cupboards, searching out antiseptic and so forth.

When she turned to face him he was clad modestly enough, in jeans, with a shirt hanging open over his chest. He held out his arm and surrendered to the pleasure of her touch as she cleansed and treated the wound.

She finished her work and began to put the things away, but he stilled her movements with a hand on her arm. 'What made you so afraid tonight? We've been at work together during storms before. It's never seemed to worry you overly much. You said just now that you couldn't bear to lose me, *too*. Who else have you lost?'

Her gaze held sorrow. 'My parents took a boat out one day and got caught in a storm a lot like this one. They drowned at sea. It was a long time ago, but since it happened I haven't been able to get rid of my aversion to deep ocean waters. Except to forget for a while that day on the island with you.'

'Hell, Claire, I'm sorry.' He'd known her parents were dead. He should have made the connection. Why hadn't he ever asked her about it? Found out the details? It explained so much, and made him realise what an ass he had been. 'And I forced you to swim in the ocean, then tried to make you come out on it with me today. Forgive me.'

When she looked into his eyes with acceptance and trust, desire flared in him. He groaned her name and reached for her. He had to have her, to hold her and keep her, so she belonged to him and never wanted to leave.

Surprise reared inside him. Had their rough beginning really shaken him that much?

'Kiss me, Claire.' Their mouths met and clung. Their bodies pressed together in deep, urgent contact.

Claire's hands plucked at his shirt, pulling it from him as he encouraged her backward into the bedroom. Their movements were a heated dance of clashing mouths and twining limbs. When her hands touched the bare flesh of his chest Nicholas forgot about the storm altogether. He sucked in a sharp breath and searched deep in her eyes for the truth that she wanted this.

It was there. Desire. Permission. Acceptance. Trust. Love?

His heart pounded at the thought. He lifted the hem of her shirt to pull it over her head. She helped him remove it. The white lace-edged bra followed quickly, and he drank in the sight of her.

'You're so beautiful. Perfect. I want you so much.'

Mouths fused again. Hot, greedy, demanding. And he found the other Claire. The one he had wondered about. The one who forgot about control and fell headlong into the moment.

Nicholas revelled in the discovery, and moments later had his wife naked on the bed beside him, the covers flung back where they wouldn't get in the way. Flesh to flesh, body to body. Finally, they would be one.

Deep gratitude and a heady neediness swept through him. His eyes prickled and he had to blink rapidly. 'You're a gift to me.' He hadn't wanted to treasure her, but somehow the feelings had caught him anyhow.

Claire's entire body burned, and everywhere that burned cried out the same thing. She wanted Nicholas. Right now. She wanted this one chance to give all of herself to him, holding back nothing. To love him with her body and her heart and her soul. *For tonight I'm his and he is mine.*

All other conscious thought left her as she reached for him, lifted her arms and her body to him in desperate, mindless surrender. 'Make love to me.'

'I'm going to love you until you ache.' He ran his hands down her sides, shaping her waist, the curve of her hips.

'I already ache.' Her laugh was hoarse, needy. She floated outside herself, all negative thought suspended. She just wanted him to take her. 'I can't think of anything else.'

His smile was triumphant and tender, and oh, so sweet. It made her insides flip all over again.

Nicholas proceeded to lavish attention on her body, tiny piece by tiny piece, until there wasn't a place that remained on her that he hadn't reverenced.

His gentleness was in direct counterpoint to the fury of the storm outside. She tried to drag herself out of the whirlpool he was creating so she could love his body in like fashion, but he quickly stopped her.

'Next time.' His grin was crooked, steeped in a hard-edged neediness that would remain locked in her mind and heart for ever—because this was for her. All for her. 'I want to make this last for you. To make it special. With your hands on me that way I can't promise even to control myself.'

That admission did something to Claire. Broke something down inside her. With a near-sob of desire she arched upward, inviting his pleasuring. Whatever he wanted to do to her or with her, she wanted it too. And she repeated the litany in breathless whispers and sobbing pleas. *Make love to me.*

As the storm ebbed, their passion soared. Loving Nicholas was the most exquisite, soul-shattering, unparallelled experience of her life. When he finally found his release in her she clutched him close, still flying on her own fulfilment. Awe filled her, and tears rushed to her eyes.

He looked at her at that moment, and kissed the tears away. Although he was breathless, his arms shaking as he stayed poised above her, he offered that crooked smile again. 'Thank you for the sweetest, most memorable experience of my life.'

It seemed he might say more, but he stopped, and his throat worked before he buried his face in the crook of her neck and placed a gentle kiss there.

In that moment Claire's heart left her body and handed itself over to him. She would never be the same.

'Thank *you*, Nicholas.' Her hands stroked the long planes of his back, his sweat-sheened shoulders. She ached to tell him she loved him, but those words couldn't be said. Instead she told him with her touch, with the press of her mouth against his skin.

They fell asleep in each other's arms, their bodies twined together in the darkness as the last remnants of the storm ebbed to a standstill outside.

What wreckage had been left behind?

CHAPTER TEN

WORK. The panacea for all ills, or so they said. Claire was at the office and buried to the neck in it by seven-thirty on Monday morning. But it hadn't achieved the numbing effect she wanted.

Whenever she turned and caught a glimpse of Nicholas's empty office, she thought of the way he had made love to her last night. Each time rain pattered against the outer office windows, she remembered the scent of it on his skin when he came in soaked from the storm, and the gentle way he had touched her, almost as though he loved her. Well, that was getting into the realms of fantasy, a place she had no purpose in going.

Face it. Her personal life was a mess. Why else had she snuck from the house so early all by herself? And now there were work issues to contend with as well. Nicholas would be very angry when he found out what was happening with the Campbell installation, but he must be told. And the sooner, the better.

Drumming her fingers on the desktop, she glared at the phone. She had hoped to have a bit of time to herself before she had to face him, but that had all changed now. She needed to speak to him, and she hadn't been able to raise him at the house.

She snatched the phone up and tried again. The answering machine picked up. Again. She'd left a message earlier. Claire hung up and sat with her eyes closed, head tipped forward, elbows on the desk, as she massaged her temples with her fingertips.

You shouldn't have made love with him.

Great. The voice of her conscience had stirred into noisy life again. She had been free of it for—what?—a whole minute just now?

So, fine. I know I did the wrong thing, but I also know what to do now. I keep my distance from Nicholas until I pay the blackmailer off, and then I get out, myself.

Only the talk was pure bravado. She didn't have the faintest notion how to achieve any of it.

She didn't hear the lift ping, had barely registered the meaning of the footsteps approaching, before Nicholas strode through the room into his office.

'Come in here, Claire. Talk to me about this Campbell situation.' He slung his briefcase onto one of the spare seats and threw himself into his desk chair.

'You got my message?'

'I was in the shower when you called. You left very early this morning. I expected to find you still in bed beside me when I woke up.' For a split second his mouth tightened on the criticism, then he went on. 'Is this the file? Tell me what's happened while I look through it.'

'Okay.' Claire was eager to get into business—particularly if it meant avoiding any expansion on that momentary black look. Why borrow trouble before she had to? 'You know John Greaves is taking care of this account? I phoned him at home, too, and asked him to get in here as fast as he could.'

John Greaves hadn't sounded particularly co-operative. 'I didn't mention the reason, just that you wanted to see him ASAP.'

Nicholas nodded. 'John checked each of the sites late last week and gave me a clear report on all of them. He said the systems were ready to run.'

'Unfortunately, his all-clear was incorrect.' Claire explained the problem as concisely as she could. 'Everything went okay at first. It was when the Campbell Group shifted the systems to the weekend security settings. Problems broke out at one site after another.'

'Why didn't they contact us? Why didn't our own people let me know there was a problem?'

'Campbells say they've been in contact with John, and our security people...' She paused.

'Yes?' His brows came down into a formidable vee.

Claire drew a deep breath. 'Our security people say they were instructed to report only to John Greaves.'

Nicholas punched a button on his phone system. 'John.' His tone was deceptively mild. 'Glad you're in. Come and see me, please.' He paused. 'Yes. Right now would be good.'

Claire rose gratefully to leave his office.

'By the way...' His words drew her to a stop.

She pivoted on the heels of her black pumps. 'Yes?'

'You and I are due for a discussion too.' His look was every bit as hawk-like as she had ever seen it, and something more besides. A shiver passed down her spine. He gave a feral smile and went on. 'It's just in abeyance until this other mess is sorted out.'

'Then I'll get on with some work.' Her words were calm, but inside she was shaking.

After last night's shattering lovemaking, she wasn't ready to address anything to do with their relationship. He had given her one beautiful experience. It was going to have to last her a lifetime. And that thought broke her heart.

Claire was trying to be strong, but she felt torn right down the middle. Stripped of all her protective mechanisms and utterly exposed. She desperately needed time to gather her resources again, but at best she was likely to get only a few measly minutes.

John Greaves was with Nicholas for almost an hour, as it happened. Not that Claire felt any better for the time spent by herself. Her thoughts simply whirled around in circles, getting nowhere.

At intervals she heard John's raised voice blustering behind Nicholas's closed door, but at no time did Nicholas's voice rise above its usual regulated tones. That fact concerned her more than if he had ranted and raved as well.

Would he take that cold, deadly tone with her when they talked? Would he flatly tell her that her period of abstinence was well and truly over now, and he expected her to make her body available to him whenever it suited?

He's not a barbarian.

No, but he was strong, determined—and, when it suited him to be, very difficult to resist.

When John Greaves emerged from the office, Claire glanced at him once, then turned her attention back to her typing. That one glance had been enough to show her a face paled to chalky-white, a mouth held in a tight line. Clearly *that* meeting had not gone well.

Nicholas made a couple of phone calls before he called her back into his office. She braced herself for the worst.

Instead of the onslaught she expected, he rose from behind the desk, took her in his arms, and buried his face in her hair for a long moment before he reluctantly released her.

'I wanted to make sure things are all right with you this morning, but there's no time.' He stepped away and pushed his hands deep into his trouser pockets. 'I have to go away, Claire. This Campbell mess is urgent, and I'm going to be relying on you to take care of everything else while I see what I can salvage of it.'

The reprieve she so desperately needed had been handed to her on a plate. 'What do you want me to do? What's happening with John Greaves?'

'He's out.' Claire had thought he was calm, but for a moment all his anger rose to the surface. 'There are very few things in life that I really can't stand, but deceit tops the list. It's inexcusable. Greaves replaced some of the quoted components on the Campbell job with inferior materials.' His voice continued, relentlessly recounting the list of Greaves's faults. 'He then pocketed the difference in costs for his own benefit. Bookmaker bills, apparently. He has lied to my face on countless occasions, deliberately misled me for his own purposes. And the man regretted being caught, but showed no true remorse.'

Each word he spoke drove a nail into Claire's heart, for he could have been describing her own behaviour towards him. She opened her mouth. To beg? To plead? She didn't know. But he flicked a hand in a weary gesture that silenced her before she said a word.

'The only thing that would give me pleasure now would be an assurance that I'd never have to clap eyes on him again.'

Claire blinked back tears, her heart in her throat and breaking there. 'I'm so sorry, Nicholas.'

He shook his head, then gave that crooked smile that was so endearing. Her control slipped even further.

'I'm usually better at managing my anger,' he said. 'But talking to you is so easy I forget myself and let it all rip.'

'Nicholas, I have to tell you—'

'These are the things I need you to do—' He spoke at the same time, and stopped abruptly. 'If something's troubling you...?'

'No.' She shook her head. It was too late now to confess. Far, far too late. And in her heart, she knew it. It was just as well he had stopped her before she got that far. 'No, nothing is troubling me except that I want to help you salvage the Campbell situation. Tell me what I have to do while you're gone.'

He gave her a list that would keep her on her toes for days, and followed it up with a searing kiss that burned her conscience as much as it touched her soul.

'I won't call.' His mouth quirked just the tiniest bit as he held her loosely in his arms. 'We'll both be busy, and I'd rather focus on getting things done and getting back here, but I'll carry the memory of making love to you. I hope you will, too.'

She closed her eyes and pressed her face into his chest, overwhelmed because her heart was too full—and too broken. 'I'll never forget it.'

Nicholas held on for long moments, then finally released her. He glanced at his watch, looking torn. 'I have to go.'

'Yes.' Claire drew a shuddering breath. 'Good luck. I'll do my best with everything for you at this end.'

'Claire?' His gaze devoured her. 'When I come back—'

'We'll install a Jacuzzi on the balcony.' She tried to smile, but had never felt more vulnerable. 'And fix up the flowerbeds in your garden. We'll get on with our fairytale marriage.'

Why had she even said it?

Again, he hesitated. Then he shook his head. 'Yes. We will.'

He stuffed some documents into his briefcase, and left the office without looking back.

The phone rang minutes after Nicholas had left. With her thoughts still on her husband— a husband in truth now, though that only made matters more complicated—Claire picked up the handset. 'This is Claire.'

'You have a caller on line one,' the receptionist's chirpy voice informed her.

It had better not be some telemarketer again. The receptionists had been warned to screen calls properly.

Claire punched a button. 'Mr Monroe's office. Claire speaking.'

'And how lovely it is to hear your sweet, sunny voice.'

Haynes. The hairs on the back of Claire's neck stood up. She clenched her hand around the receiver. 'What do you want? How did you get this number? Why are you calling me?'

Sophie's ex-boss gave a harsh laugh. 'Things have changed. You're married to Monroe now. It's not like you can't afford to pay me, so I've decided you will. This Friday. Same time. Same place. Same method.'

There was a chilling pause, and Claire could hear him breathing harshly on the other end of the line.

'Let me down,' he said, 'and you'll be sorry.'

Claire gasped. 'You can't do that. I don't *have* the money. What are you saying?'

But it was too late. The blackmailer had hung up. Claire replaced the phone gingerly. She had the weirdest sense that if she wasn't careful Haynes would somehow climb through it to hurt her.

Her rational mind told her that was silly, but her gut instinct was screaming that the man was on edge in an unhealthy way. For long moments she sat, her mind whirling, fear churning her stomach.

There was no choice. She had to get the money right now. It was ironic, really. Before the wedding she had *wanted* to pay off the blackmailer but hadn't been able to get the money. Now, because she was Nicholas's wife, she would be able to use his name to get a loan and she didn't want to have to do it.

Because once she paid Haynes off, her marriage would be over.

The rest of the week passed too quickly. Before she knew it Claire was standing in Greenhaul Park, across from the Monroe offices, her senses itching with some indefinable unease.

The grounds bustled with lunchtime traffic. Walkers, joggers, mothers with small children, teenagers playing hookey from school. And all sorts of office workers, taking time out from their busy days. They sat on park benches or sprawled on the lawns, eating gourmet deli sandwiches or box lunches bought from nearby cafés and other food outlets.

Claire came here often to eat her lunch. A fact that the blackmailer knew and had taken advantage of in the past. Today she watched the Friday ebb and flow of people with her heart in shreds.

She'd got the money. Had used the fact that she was Nicholas's wife to secure a bank loan that would have had her laughed off the premises before. If she couldn't pay it back the bank would go to her husband for payment, so it looked as if all her wages would go towards paying off the loan even after she'd left Monroe's.

At least once this meeting was over the blackmailer would be paid off at last. Claire would be glad about that, because with each encounter he became more creepy.

Once she got him out of her life Claire would leave Monroe's for ever. Today, before Nicholas returned. He would be angry and hurt when she walked out of his life, and that knowledge hurt her in turn, because she had let herself fall in love with him.

Stupid, stupid thing to do. He hadn't changed. He didn't love her now any more than he had when he proposed marriage. Their lovemaking had pleased him, but his emotions were still his own. That would never change.

It's the right thing. It would kill me to stay with him, knowing he doesn't share my feelings.

How could she stay, anyway, knowing she had deceived him from the start? If she tried to explain he would hate her, and she couldn't bear that either.

She watched for Gordon Haynes with a heavy heart, and promised herself when this meeting ended she would go straight back to the office and pen her goodbyes. A resignation as both his employee and his wife. It was a letter she had not yet been able to write, despite her best efforts to reconcile herself to having to leave him.

At least she had taken good care of things for him in his absence, tying up every loose end she could find that needed tying. He would come back to a shipshape Monroe's, at least as far as his own part of the business was concerned.

Claire even had her eye on a suitable successor for the personal assistant's slot. The woman who had filled in the week they'd become engaged would probably jump at the chance if invited to step into the space until Nicholas's regular assistant returned at the end of her sick leave.

Tears prickled at the backs of Claire's eyes and she blinked them back in annoyance. She mustn't cry. Not now. Because Haynes was approaching, his movements jerky as he stepped towards her.

When he drew level Claire handed over the plastic shopping bag that bore the mark of a nearby bookstore. The cash was taped inside an empty book cover in the bag. She tried not to meet his gaze, but could feel his eyes boring into her.

'Here it is, packaged the same as last time.'

Haynes took the bag, glanced inside, and gave a soft, satisfied laugh that made her want to hurry away as fast as she could. He zipped the bag into an inside pocket in his jacket.

'Very good.' His voice was almost singsong. 'I knew you'd have no trouble getting it so quickly.'

'You have no idea what I may or may not have been through to procure your *little gift*.' She snarled the words, determined to finish with him. 'Take it and go. I've done what you asked. I've given you every red cent you demanded to keep quiet about my sister. Now it's over.'

She turned away, aching to be gone from him. To be away from his corrupt, unnerving presence so she could begin to put her life back together. Only she wasn't sure she would ever be able to put it together again.

'Not quite so fast.' Haynes's tone held blatant threat now. He didn't try to hide it. But it was his touch on her arm that sent the blackest shivers down her spine.

'Take your hand off me.' She whispered the words through clenched teeth, and tugged against his hold.

He released her, but not until he'd maintained his grip for long moments, his dark eyes narrowed on her with what she swore was hatred.

What had she ever done to make him feel that way towards her?

'Don't get in a panic, *Mrs Monroe*.' His smile showed too many teeth. 'We just aren't quite finished with our business dealings, that's all.'

'We're completely finished.' She backed a step, suppressing a shudder. 'Your silence has been paid for, and I have nothing else to say to you.'

'Which suits me rather well.' His eyes hardened into dark chips. 'I'd prefer you to simply listen, anyway. And listen carefully. Because what I have to say is going to matter to you.'

She tried for brave rejection. 'I doubt that.'

Before she could take another step, he spoke. 'Oh, you'll think so, all right.'

She wanted to dismiss him, but she was caught in the aura of menace that surrounded him. 'Get on with it, then. I'm listening.'

'You and your sister have done rather well for yourselves, haven't you?' He leaned forward. 'Little Sophie, married to a senator—and now you, the wife of the head of Monroe's, no less.'

Claire didn't like him talking about her marriage, or about her sister. 'Is there a point to this?'

Haynes ran a caressing hand over his bald patch. For a moment his gaze was unfocussed, then he snapped it back to her. 'I've had a hard life, Claire, and I want reparation. You're going to give it to me.'

'No. We're finished. We had a bargain. I've given you what you wanted.' She'd wanted to sound immovable, but the words had come out thin and high-pitched.

Haynes stepped even closer, until his stale breath filled her nostrils and she wanted to gag. 'My business isn't doing well, Claire. Nobody appreciates good, simple service these days. I'm sick of it all. I want to retire some place nice. Put my feet up. Stop worrying. Seven hundred and fifty thousand dollars will buy me a nice place on the coast. Ten monthly instalments of seventy-five thousand dollars apiece. You make the first payment here, Monday lunchtime.'

Was he insane? 'I can't pay it.' She couldn't possibly get her hands on that sort of money. It simply wasn't possible. 'There's no way—'

He gripped both her shoulders and his chilling eyes raked her face. 'Find a way.'

'Or what?' Claire was quaking inside, but she forced herself to meet him stare for stare. 'You'll hurt me?'

He laughed and let her go, just a photocopier man once again. Pleasant, friendly, serene. 'Oh, no, Claire. I won't hurt *you*. I'll hurt your husband—the man behind the money. A drive-by shooting, perhaps? They're getting quite commonplace in certain areas of Sydney these days. Or maybe he'll go to cross the street outside his office one day and get hit by a passing car. What a tragedy it would be. What a waste of a good life.'

He meant it. She didn't want to believe it, but the truth was there in his eyes. This man was unhinged. He thought money would solve all problems. Claire gave a bitter, silent laugh. She had certainly learned that was not the case.

She stepped towards him. 'Please—'

'Monday.' He cut her off. 'See that you do it.'

He melted away through the crowd, and Claire stood looking after him, quaking. He had threatened to kill Nicholas. How could she get her hands on that amount of money? What could she do?

She didn't know how long she stood, staring into space, before a voice behind whipped her from her reverie. A very familiar, very much loved and wonderful voice. A voice she had never expected to hear again.

She whirled. 'Nicholas!'

CHAPTER ELEVEN

NICHOLAS returned early from his trip with a single thought in mind. He wanted to see Claire. She often went to the park opposite for her breaks, and luckily he'd found her there, standing next to a park bench. She flung herself into his arms with an incoherent cry and he hauled her in close and simply enjoyed the feel of her arms twined around his waist.

After a moment, a shudder passed through her, and she tipped her head up to search his face. 'Nicholas. You're well? You're all right? I'm so glad to see you.'

'I'm fine. No storms to survive this time,' he quipped, but then he sobered. 'I missed you.' The words escaped him without conscious thought. At the clenching of her fingers against him his senses had leapt into fully wakened desire. He wanted her. Desperately, thoroughly, right now.

219

'I missed you, too.' She raised her hands to his shoulders. Her gaze searched his face as though to assure herself he was really there. 'It's been a long week. I'm happy to have you back safe and sound.'

'Safe as a Monroe security system.' The wry quote didn't make her smile as he'd expected. Instead, her mouth trembled. What was that all about?

He kissed the vulnerable line of her lips with gentleness at first, but as Claire responded the kiss became more ardent. Before he could completely forget their surroundings, he broke away. 'Come back to the office. There are too many people milling around here.'

'I agree. We shouldn't stay here.' She linked her arm through his, her gaze darting this way and that as they made their way back into their building. It was almost as if she were herding him.

Nicholas shrugged. He was happy to take silent pleasure in their closeness. He nodded to the various office workers who greeted them inside the building, but was only really aware of the woman at his side.

In other circumstances he would have suggested Claire bring him up to date on work issues, and then filled her in on his own progress. Right now nothing could be further from his mind. He wanted to get her alone.

The moment he closed his office door behind them, he tugged her close and planted his mouth firmly over hers.

Heat spiralled outward in every direction until his body was suffused with it. Did she respond to his desperation? Or did they bring out the neediness in each other? He didn't know, and he wasn't sure he cared.

Something deep in the heart of him needed to be with her. To get as close as it was humanly possible to be. Maybe then the churning inside would cease and he could find some peace.

'Let me touch you.' His fingers plucked buttons from their holes until he could lay her bare beneath the sides of the blouse. In moments he had his hands on her, had the silk of her skin beneath his fingertips.

'We shouldn't do this. What if someone walked in?' She panted the words even as her hands hurried to throw off his jacket and strip his shirt away.

'I've locked the door.' He pulled her back towards the desk, unwilling to let her go even for a moment. With one hand he tugged the phone cord until it pulled free of its moorings. 'That takes care of any other interruptions we might have.'

Claire's groan was half yielding, half denial, but her mouth held desperation and hungry heat as it met his.

The room was still, the soft muted hum of the air-conditioner the only sound aside from panting breaths and muttered sighs. If he didn't bury himself in her in seconds, he would go mad.

He tugged at her skirt, his sole thought to get it off her, out of the way. Then he drew a breath and forced himself to slow down.

It seemed Claire wanted none of that. 'Hurry, hurry.' Her hands pulled at his belt, then swept his hands aside from the zip of her skirt to try and help him remove the garment.

Her need filled him with a sense of power, and doubled his need for her. With a muffled growl, he freed her of the rest of her clothes and shed his own.

'Protection.' She mumbled the word into his chest.

In their haste the other night they hadn't used any, and when he'd questioned her as they lay together afterwards, Claire had said it was too early in her cycle to be likely to cause a problem.

'I'll take care of it.' He swept her into his arms and over to the sofa, snatching his wallet from his trousers as he went. In moments he was poised above her, eager to spin out the pleasure as long as he could for both of them.

'You're more beautiful every time I look at you.' And he did look, taking in every part of her from the crown of her head to her toes.

She blushed, and her hands sank into the hair at his nape, her fingers sliding sensually against him there. 'You're beautiful, too. The most beautiful man I've ever seen or known.'

Heat rose to his cheeks. To cover it, he gave a wry, teasing smile. 'Seen a whole lot, have you?'

'You know what I meant.' She swatted his shoulder.

His smile faded and he looked deep into her eyes, relishing the fire he saw there, the hunger that was for him. All for him.

'Yes. I know what you meant, and I thank you for the sentiment. Now, let me show you what *I* mean. What I'm thinking about right now, and what I want to do to you and with you.'

The last time they'd made love it had been gentle, the room shadowed by the night, the storm playing itself out beyond the walls. He hadn't been able to see her fully, nor to hear every tiny sound she made.

This time he could see and hear with total clarity, and he took advantage and enjoyed both to the fullest. Her skin was honey-gold and smooth as silk, with tiny freckles here and there. When he stroked his hands down the length of her arms to her fingertips she caught her breath.

She writhed, arching upward, her desire as clear as her movements. He kissed her neck, her mouth, gentled her with nibbling kisses.

His breath rasped. Deep within, he ached for her welcome, for the release she would bring him—that they would find together. 'Fall with me, Claire. Leap over the edge with me.'

They climbed until there was nowhere left to climb, and when they reached that pinnacle they hovered there, breathlessly alive and dying at one and the same time.

Choked with emotion, unable to speak past the rawness in his throat, he collapsed in her arms.

The weekend passed, but it was far from peaceful. Claire was so deep into trouble she wondered if it really could get any worse.

Just before lunchtime on Monday, when she had to meet Haynes to pay the seventy-five thousand dollars, she made an excuse to leave the office, found a homeless man at the edge of the park, and gave him a picture of Haynes that she'd printed from Haynes's business website. She also handed the man an envelope containing the typed, unsigned note she wanted him to deliver.

I need time. I can't pay that much at once. I'll meet you here a month from today, with ten thousand dollars. We'll talk again then.

Haynes's intimidation campaign started the day after. He phoned her at work. Loitered outside her favourite sandwich bar when she went to grab lunch for her and Nicholas. All his threats were targeted at her husband's safety.

Claire changed her routine. Stayed away from her regular haunts. Refused to take phone calls at work unless she recognised the name of the caller.

At the end of the month, on the allotted day, she maxed out her cash advance option on a new credit card and paid Haynes ten thousand dollars. He took the money, but was incensed that she hadn't paid the full amount.

Claire made the mistake of begging for Nicholas's safety, and Haynes used it. Now, in six days, Haynes expected her to pay the remaining sixty-five thousand dollars on threat of Nicholas's life.

She wished she could tell Nicholas everything. Confess and ask him to help her. But if she did he would know she had deceived him from the start. He would push her out of his life, and then Haynes would have free access to him. And Haynes was so angry Claire didn't doubt he would carry out his threat to kill Nicholas.

Claire couldn't risk it. So she watched Nicholas, and she planned. She would take more money on the payment day, whatever she could scrape up, and she would work on Haynes. She would convince him to let her pay smaller amounts over a longer period and get him to agree that he wouldn't hurt Nicholas. Ever.

At least she had a plan, but the long hours of watching over Nicholas, and the anxiety, had taken their toll on Claire. For days now she had been physically sick with worry.

On cue, her stomach began to churn. If someone had told her she could worry herself into actual nausea and vomiting she would have laughed, but it had happened. So far she had hidden the worst from Nicholas, but that effort, too, was wearing her down.

Today they were out in the backyard in the sunshine, working on the side flower borders that filled the large tree-canopied area. Claire was grateful for the chance to try to relax a bit.

'I feel terribly guilty, letting you do all the hard work while I sit here in comfort just watching.' From her position on the outdoor lounger chair, she fanned her face.

Nicholas straightened from beside one of the borders. In his denim shorts and navy shirt he looked cool and comfortable. They shouldn't be doing these sorts of things at all. Making inroads into a future that wasn't real. Claire worried about that, too.

'No need to feel guilty. You've pitched in a lot of the time.' He smiled to match the carefree tone, but concern showed in his gaze as it travelled over her. 'When you shake off this fluey feeling it will be soon enough for me to demand total slave rights.'

'Oh, *hah*. As if I'd let you make a slave of me.' The flu theory was as good an excuse as any other. For that reason, she'd run with it when he'd first said it.

'Not even if I asked you to do Jacuzzi duty?' He waggled his eyebrows. 'Scrub my back? Bring me champagne? That wouldn't be too onerous a slave task, would it?'

'I suppose you'd expect strawberries, too?' She said it without thinking, and her heart stabbed at the piquant memories of her first visit here, when Nicholas had shown her the balcony and she had blurted all those ideas. 'But the Jacuzzi isn't ready yet. They told us to leave it a few more days to be certain the surrounds set properly.'

'Yes, I know.' He pushed the last plant into the ground, patted it down, and gave it a dose of water from the hose at his side. 'Blame it on the warm day and the exercise. The idea of sinking up to my neck in cool water appeals right now.'

As he straightened, he dusted his hands off in a no-nonsense sort of way. 'What would make you feel great right now? A long, cool drink? An ice cream? There has to be something. Tell me what it is.'

Your guaranteed safety and a searing kiss. The latter thought sprang from nowhere, reminding her that they had shared kisses and much, much more these past few weeks.

Memories. Surely I'm entitled to memories to take with me when it's safe to leave him?

She dropped her gaze, in case he should read the angst in her eyes.

'Fruit sorbet.' The thought of something fruity and cold was refreshing. 'Maybe I'll have some juice when we go inside.'

'And maybe we should go out and buy sorbet.' He tugged her up from the lounger chair, hugged her, and let go.

The contact was friendly, tender, *sweet*. He was so many things she hadn't expected ever to know. Right now as he looked at her his eyes sparkled with good humour and she wasn't sure what else.

'Give me two minutes to wash the dirt off and change shoes,' he said, 'and we'll go.'

She couldn't beg him to stay home, where she felt most confident about ensuring his safety, but she would watch over him.

'Okay.' By the time she started to follow, he was halfway to the house. 'Where exactly are we going?' She called the question to his retreating back. 'I'm not sure I even know where we can find sorbet around here.'

His shrug was full of Nicholas confidence. 'We'll figure something out.'

True to his word, he was ready to leave in minutes, his canvas shoes an echo of the ones she had on her own feet, a fresh shirt pulled over his muscled chest.

Claire knew that chest intimately now, knew exactly how firm and solid it was, and how the heart within hammered when his need for her was greatest.

She forced back a groan and gave herself a stern admonition to think of something else. The street out front was quiet. No cars. Claire wanted to hustle him, but forced herself to appear calm.

When they reached the twin garage, he opened a different door from usual, revealing a deep green sedan inside. She drew back in surprise, then moved forward to inspect the vehicle. Once she had tugged Nicholas inside with her, she relaxed enough to look the car over.

'Wow. That's one seriously nice vehicle. Whose is it? Where'd it come from?'

Nicholas just looked at her, smiling. After a long moment he laughed, reached for her hand, and dropped a set of keys into it. 'Surprise. It's yours—from me. I hope you really do like it.'

He was giving her a car? Just like that? Every time she thought she had his measure, he surprised her all over again. She wasn't sure how many more surprises she could take.

'You didn't say a word about this.' Her throat closed up. She stared at him, speechless, then stared at the car. Finally she found her voice. 'You can't just buy me a car.'

'Yeah, I can. It's as easy as going out on a sunny Saturday to buy sorbet. That's the idea of a surprise, by the way. Keeping it quiet until you're ready to spring it on the recipient.' He gestured to the driver's side. 'Jump in. Let's put her through her paces.'

Slowly, Claire got into the car, buckled her seatbelt, went through the motions of locating blinkers, wipers, horn, et cetera. In the middle of it she turned to him. 'Nicholas—'

'I know. I'm a great guy, and you're glad you married me.' He leaned across the space that separated them and bestowed a swift kiss on her mouth. 'I'm glad I married you, too.'

More money spent on her. More guilt added to her load. To cover the sudden ache in her heart, she started the car and backed it out of the garage. 'So...' She gave it a gentle rev, just because Nicholas was a guy and she figured he would have done so in her place. 'We're buying sorbet. Which way shall we go?'

As she drove towards the city, she kept a close watch on the vehicles around them, checking that they weren't being followed by Haynes. They made it safely enough, though, and she parked the car with relief.

They got out and started to walk. Claire kept an eye out as Nicholas led the way to a quiet restaurant. When they stepped inside and she saw the plushness of the place she raised her eyebrows at him.

'I'm not sure they'll even let us in. We're not exactly dressed for it.'

In fact, there were very few patrons. The lunch crowd was long gone, the dinner crowd not yet started. And if the hostess thought anything of their casual attire, she kept it to herself.

Once they were seated, well away from the front plate glass windows, Claire smiled across the small table at Nicholas. 'It was my pseudo-silk shirt that got us through. It quite made up for your lack of collar and tie.'

'Are you saying it wasn't my charming smile that did it?' He turned the smile in question onto the young waitress as she approached with pen and pad poised. The girl promptly blushed to the roots of her hair before stammering out a request for their order.

'Peach sorbet, please.' Claire cast a frowning glance at Nicholas.

He raised innocent eyebrows and shrugged. 'I'll have the same. Thanks.'

After the girl left, Claire shook her head at him. 'That wasn't very nice. Your smile is lethal, you know. Using it on her like that, you've probably given her a permanent case of the stutters.'

Nicholas was silent for a second, then he shook his head. 'You're good for me, Claire, but I don't suppose it's occurred to you that you overrate my charms?'

She started to laugh, then realised he was serious. The smile died on her lips. 'You're a very attractive man, Nicholas, and I mean *very* attractive. When you smile in that certain way you have, I have no choice. I melt at your feet. It's that simple. Trust me, I know what I'm talking about.'

Claire hadn't meant to bring the conversation to such a sensual level, but the darkening of his eyes and her own erratic breathing confirmed it had happened anyway.

With effort, she caught her breath and brought her flaring emotions under control. She was in love with this man, and as the weeks passed he seemed to grow closer to her, too.

If only...

But there was too much between them. Too many deceptions. Nicholas valued honesty and straightforwardness, and from her he'd got neither from the start. And he would never love her. Not ever.

'I'm no more interesting to look at than any number of other men.'

'I suppose that's true.' She forced the dark thoughts aside and focussed on this conversation, right now. How could she explain his appeal? Maybe loving him coloured her opinion, but she didn't think so. *Everything* about Nicholas drew her, lured her.

'Your character reveals itself in your smile, in your expressions. You're strong, kind, generous, and that shows through. Just look at the way you've spoiled me these last ten days or so.'

'You're worth spoiling.' He lifted her hand to kiss the fingertips.

For a man who didn't believe in love, he did a good job of making her feel cared for and wanted.

Their sorbets arrived and she took a deep breath, gently disengaged her hand, and turned the conversation to a discussion of the car's performance. As was so often the case lately, Nicholas seemed to sense her need to lighten things up, and shifted to the new topic without so much as a blink.

As they talked, she relaxed. It gave her pleasure to watch the expressions move across his face as he enthused about various aspects of car anatomy. She smiled, enjoying him, until he rambled to a stop.

His mouth pulled into a wry twist. 'You've got no idea what I'm on about, have you?'

She shook her head, still smiling. 'Nope. None whatsoever.'

'Nor do you care.' His lips twitched, giving away his amusement.

'I do *care*.' She cast around for a way to explain the difference between caring about a car and *caring* in the way guys did, with their polishing and waxing and spritzing and sprucing. 'I just don't really—'

'*Care*, care. I get it.' He looked ready to tease her further on the topic, but his cellphone started to chirp. He lifted it from his shorts pocket to look at it. 'Hmm. That's Forrester.'

'Answer it.' Claire flapped her hand at the instrument. 'It could be important.'

Nicholas smiled and pressed a button on the phone. 'Monroe.'

Claire eavesdropped without the slightest compunction. The conversation wasn't lengthy, but the gist was clear.

The moment Nicholas ended the call, she leaped to her feet. 'We got the deal! We got the deal!'

The few other patrons in the establishment turned their heads, some smiling at her obvious exuberance. She ignored them, grabbing Nicholas by the hands and squeezing hard.

'I'm so proud. I knew they'd choose Monroe's, because Monroe's is the best. *You're* the best. Didn't I tell you? *Didn't* I?'

'Yes, you told me.' Nicholas smiled at his wife's display of exuberance. 'I think we're about finished here. Let's go home.' He tossed several notes onto the table, and escorted her to the door.

A feeling of light-heartedness stole over him. Not because he had closed the Forrester deal at last, but because for once Claire was smiling without a sign of shadows in her eyes.

These past weeks had been hard on her. He wasn't entirely certain why. Was it just a slump in her overall health? Or was something deeper bothering her? He didn't want to believe Claire was less than happy in case that led him to wonder if she was less than happy in some way *with him.*

Over the weeks it had become important that she *was* happy. Totally and utterly happy. He hadn't expected to feel quite so strongly about that. Occasionally he asked himself if this meant he could be hurt, in the same way his father had been.

But he would shake his head, rejecting the idea. Claire was honest to the bone, kind and straight dealing. She was no manipulator—unlike his mother. He had made a certain kind of peace with his mother over the years, but the scars were still there.

'Would you like to drive home?' Her suggestion held a hint of knowingness.

'I could be persuaded to give the car a run.' He held out his hand for the keys with a bored air that he knew wouldn't fool her for a moment. The car had been delivered directly from the showroom and, frankly, he itched to put it through its paces.

Partway home, Claire developed that overly wide-eyed look she got when she was struggling to stay awake. He shot her a quick glance. 'You can snooze if you want to. It wouldn't be the first time I've driven you around while you slept.'

She suddenly straightened and looked around guiltily. 'I'll stay awake and keep you company.'

From the set of her chin, he could see she didn't intend to be swayed from that position. He promised himself that when they got home he would encourage her to take a nap. Even if it meant lying down with her.

His body responded predictably to that idea, and he gave a rueful inward shake of his head. *Sleep only. She'd be too tired for anything else right at this moment.*

He would lie beside Claire while she slept and thoroughly enjoy the experience. He knew it, and in fact had done exactly that a couple of times when he'd woken early in the morning. Of course, then he would wait until she began to stir, and love her awake the rest of the way…

'One-track mind.'

Her head turned towards him. 'Hmm?'

Claire slept. When she woke, Nicholas was watching her. He kissed her, and one kiss led to another, until he was loving her so slowly and gently she wept with the sheer wonder of it. Of what he could make her feel, and the look in his eyes when he moved deep within her.

Afterwards, she curled her body into his back, her arm snug around his waist, her face pressed against his shoulder blades. This was home, the place and the feeling she had waited for all her life. It would be hers for the blinking of an eye and then it would be gone. But for this moment, she would take it and be glad.

His breathing deepened and evened, and only then did she open her mouth to whisper, 'I love you, Nicholas. If nothing else, please at least know that I do love you.'

With a shuddering sigh, Claire slept again.

CHAPTER TWELVE

ON THE Monday morning after they had worked on the flower borders, three things happened to Claire. She woke to the realisation that her breasts were tender and uncomfortable, she had to run for the bathroom the moment she rolled over, only just making it to the toilet bowl before she lost the contents of her stomach.

And she realised she hadn't had a period in too long.

At three in the afternoon of the same day she was standing in Nicholas's empty office. She read the note she had written again.

I need to go home early today. Hope you don't mind. I'll catch up any work tomorrow. Claire.

With shaking hands, she tucked the note under the side of the blotter on Nicholas's desk,

242

where he would see it when he got back, and acknowledged that this was the coward's way out.

Right now she couldn't face him, so she was bolting, before he got back from his business meeting. *Time. I just need a little time to myself, then I'll be okay. I'll know exactly what to do.*

She hurried to the lift and pressed the button for the underground car park. Fortunately she had the elevator to herself, because she didn't think she could have handled company right now. Leaning her head back against the wall, she closed her eyes. *I should have realised. All the signs were there. Why didn't I see? Why weren't we more careful that first time?*

It was too late for recriminations or regrets. She was pregnant with Nicholas's child. Even as the thought blared through her head again she laid a protective, wondering hand over her belly. Panic flooded her system, but she fought it down.

I will work this out. And, drat it, she couldn't help the feeling of awe that rose in her at the thought that a new life was forming within her even now. A totally innocent, brand-new human being, made by her and Nicholas together.

A surge of love shockwaved through her. *I'll look after you, baby. No matter what, I promise I'll look after you.*

She had visited the gynaecologist in her lunch hour, and, though it was early to go home, she couldn't have stayed another minute at the office if her life had depended on it.

Nicholas was across town at his meeting. He always took a security guard along, so she didn't worry about that. And he had phoned her when he got there, so she knew he was okay. But he was expected back by four. He would come straight from the meeting to the office. And she needed time to get herself together before her and Nicholas's paths crossed again.

I'll go home, sort myself out, get a plan happening... The lift doors swished open and she headed in the direction of her new green car. *Then, when I'm fully prepared—*

'I've been waiting for you, Mrs Monroe.' Gordon Haynes stepped out from the van parked beside her car, crowding her between the two vehicles in the process.

Her first thought was of her husband, but he was safe, away from here. Before she could try to get into her car and get away Haynes took her wrist in a painful grip and prised the car keys from her, to toss them with a clatter some metres away.

'What are you doing? You're hurting me.' Claire tugged out of his grasp but couldn't get away, tucked as she was between the vehicles, his body, and the wall of the parking area.

'And I'll hurt you more if you don't co-operate.' He grabbed her again. 'Get in the van. I've thought of a better way to get my money. I'm kidnapping you, Claire. Your husband will pay a nice fat ransom—far more than I was going to get from you. I'll be rich. My troubles will be over. It's perfect.'

'I'll tell.' She struggled against him. 'The police will find you. Punish you.'

'You won't be telling anything.' He started hauling her closer to the side of the van. 'You don't really think I'd let you live to tell the tale, do you?'

Oh, God. He planned to kill her. 'Sophie...Sophie will know it was you. She'll tell the police.'

'Sophie will be so scared when I let her know what's happened to you, she'll only worry that she'll be next.'

There was such chill in his tone that Claire almost stopped breathing. She started to struggle. 'I'll scream for help. You won't get away with this.'

'Go ahead and scream. Nobody will hear you.' There was mania in his laugh.

Claire looked into his eyes and realised that whatever thread had been holding him together had snapped.

'Take a look around, my dear.' He gestured with a tilt of his chin. 'The place is deserted.'

Claire wasn't going to die. Not if she had any say in it. She had to keep him talking, figure out a way to get free of him.

'How could you know that I'd be here? I never leave the office this early.'

'I expected to have to wait.' He shrugged. 'You just made this easier for me, that's all.'

'There are a number of us leaving early this afternoon,' she blustered. 'There'll be others along any second.'

He just shook his head. 'Nice try.' His mouth turned ugly. He tugged her forward until they were almost level with the yawning doorway into the van. 'Now, get in.'

'No.' Claire leaped forward and pushed at Haynes with all her might. He staggered back, but got a hand around one of her arms before she could get away. He pulled her up short with enough force to jar her from elbow to shoulder.

Claire opened her mouth and screamed, long and loud, then ground her foot down on his instep and tried to get her elbow between them to drive it into his stomach.

'Stop!' The shout came from some distance away, but she recognised it. 'Let her go!'

So, apparently, did her assailant, who hissed her husband's name amidst a string of profanities.

With a further oath, Haynes threw her back against her car. Her body whipped backwards.

Her head cracked against the window in the driver's door, and pain shattered through her.

The last thing Claire saw as she began to slide to the ground was Nicholas, sprinting towards her. Then everything went black.

'Claire!' As Nicholas rushed towards Claire a white van pulled out from beside her car and roared away. The side door was open. The van itself was nondescript, and it had mud on the plates, but he got a good look at the driver and knew he'd be able to identify him.

That was all Nicholas had time for before he dropped to his knees beside his unconscious wife. 'Oh, God, Claire. Please be all right.'

She was slumped against her car, face pale, legs crumpled beneath her. He could see no visible sign of injury, but he had seen her head whip back when the man shoved her. A gentle exploration revealed a lump at the back of her head the size of an egg. There could be concussion, internal bleeding—who knew what else?

Anger rose in him, hot and determined. He wanted to track that man down and make him pay for hurting her. Who was he? Did he know Claire? Or Nicholas himself? Was there a connection of some kind, or was it a random attack?

He pushed the thoughts aside for when he could deal with them. A security guard had raced out of the parking lot in pursuit. Nicholas hoped he'd get the guy, but the traffic was heavy out there.

'Hold on, my love. You're going to be okay.'

Could she hear him, even if only on some subconscious level? He tried to keep his voice calm, just in case, but inside he was quaking. If anything happened to her...

Circling one wrist gently, he nodded. 'Good girl. That's a nice strong pulse you've got going there.'

He kept his fingers over that life force and with his other hand whipped out his cellphone and called for an ambulance.

'The underground parking lot of the Monroe Global Security building.' He told them the address, and which part of the lot they were in. 'My wife has been attacked and thrown against a car. She's unconscious. I felt a lump on the back of her head. It's not bleeding, but I don't know what other injuries she might have.'

'Okay, sir. Don't try to move her. Just sit tight. We're on our way.'

'Please hurry.'

That call made, he contacted the police and the head of the security team in the building, alerting both to the situation and asking that they do their best to try to trace the van.

His gaze never left Claire as he made the calls. When he'd ended them he told himself not to worry. It didn't work. He was terrified for her. Terrified he would lose her. And then what would there be? Yawning black nothingness.

He'd been stupid, hadn't he? Imagining he could bring Claire into his life and not care about her. Not let his feelings get involved with her. Not *love* her.

Stupid, arrogant fool. That's what you are. It's a wonder she ever agreed to marry you. Had his attitude forced Claire to try to suppress her feelings? Her emotions? *Of course it did. You told her those were the terms, remember?*

'When you wake up, Claire, we need to have a long talk.' He prayed she would wake up. Would be okay.

The ambulance arrived. The trip to the hospital was nightmarish. Nicholas drove behind the ambulance with his gaze glued to the rear of the vehicle and spent the time muttering under his breath for them to hurry up, although they were going quite fast already.

'What's happening? Where are they taking her?' Once inside the hospital, he tried to follow the gurney along the corridor, but was quickly stopped.

'The lady will be looked after, sir. You need to go to Admissions and get her paperwork organised.'

Who cared about paperwork? His jaw worked over the explosive words he wanted to utter, but he controlled himself somehow.

'I'm Nicholas Monroe, Monroe Global Security Systems. She's my wife. See that she has the best of care. Anything she needs. No expense spared.'

His words were met with a frosty glare, the implication being that they *always* gave their patients the best of care, whoever they might happen to be.

Duly chastened, Nicholas mumbled an apology and took himself off to Admissions to get Claire signed in. But the impatience didn't leave him. He wanted to be with her, to stand at her side and check for himself that everything possible was being done for her.

In fact over an hour passed before he got any information of use. When a doctor finally presented himself in the waiting room and called Nicholas's name, he leaped from his chair, ready to tear the man apart if he didn't have the answers Nicholas wanted to hear—and *right now*!

'How is she? What's happening? It's been sixty-five minutes and I've heard nothing. Absolutely nothing.'

'Your wife is going to be fine.' The doctor observed him with shrewd eyes, then gave a slight shake of his head. 'If you'll step this way, I'll take you to her and explain our findings.'

Action at last. Nicholas strode beside the doctor purposefully. If his legs were shaking, nobody need know about it but him.

'Mrs Monroe is in here.' The doctor opened the door to a private room.

In some part of his mind Nicholas registered that they were on a regular ward, not in Acute Care or a high dependency unit. But he couldn't and wouldn't relax until he'd looked Claire over for himself, and heard every detail of her examination and current state from the man at his side.

The moment he entered the room his gaze honed in on the bed. Claire lay there, eyes closed. Her face was leached of all colour. She had been changed into a hospital gown, and had the uniform cellular blanket tucked up beneath her chin.

Her eyes opened, and she smiled faintly. 'Nicholas. They told me you got me here.'

'You're awake.' He crossed the room and grasped her hand. If ever he had craved physical contact to this degree before, he couldn't remember when. 'How do you feel?'

'My head hurts, and I feel a bit queasy. But it's not so bad.'

The doctor began to talk through the process of care from admission to now. Nicholas's gaze never left Claire's face as he listened. She had taken quite a knock, but for all that, they were confident there was nothing worse than mild concussion.

The doctor made a joke about Claire having a hard head. Nicholas smiled dutifully, but without any trace of real humour. Maybe later he would be able to laugh about this—although the way he felt now, he doubted it.

He might have lost Claire, and he hadn't even told her that he loved her. That he couldn't face the thought of living without her.

Hell, he hadn't realised he felt this way until this had happened. Again he thought what a blind, stupid fool he had been. He loved Claire. But how did she feel about him? Where would this new discovery of his take them?

Suddenly he wanted the doctor out of the room so he could be alone with his wife. He turned to the man in time to hear his final words.

'The baby is just fine. No problems on that front.' The doctor's voice was calm and assured. 'We'll keep your wife in overnight for observation. If all goes well I expect that tomorrow you'll be able to take her home and she can complete her convalescence there.'

'Baby?' What did the doctor mean, *baby*? Nicholas's mind felt blank, as though it couldn't take in one more thing.

'All fine, as I said.' The doctor turned towards the door. 'I must go, but our staff will keep a close eye on your wife. Good day to you.'

Nicholas mumbled what he hoped were appropriate words of thanks. It seemed the least he could do. But the moment the man left the room he closed the door firmly after him and moved back to the side of the bed.

Claire looked up at him with eyes as big as saucers. 'Won't you sit down? I feel a little intimidated when you stand over me like that.'

He scraped a chair forward and sank into it, wondering where to start. 'What the doctor said...' The question burned in him. Was it true? Was there a baby on the way?

But there were other words that burned as well, and he felt they had to be spoken first.

It didn't come easily to him to confront these feelings. He had made a lifetime's work of decrying love and all it stood for. Of protecting himself from it. This marriage had been designed to give him the things he wanted *without* the emotional commitment that would be expected in a love match.

But all that had changed now, and he had to tell her, no matter what it cost him.

'I love you, Claire. Heart and soul.' He took her hand in his and bent his gaze to her slender fingers. As he searched for the right words his hold tightened. 'I didn't realise how much until I saw you struggling with that man beside your car. I'll find out who he is and see that he's punished, I promise you.'

Claire's hand fluttered in his, but she remained silent.

Nicholas took a deep breath, and went on. 'I know I said I wanted a convenient marriage, but I was wrong to ask for that when there could be so much more. I plan to win you, Claire, on every level. You may not be able to return my love at first, but I hope your feelings will grow over time.'

When she still didn't speak, he addressed the other issue.

'If we're having a baby, I want to protect our child, too, and give it a true family. A happy, loving family. I hope you'll say there's a chance for all that for us, Claire. For something more than the business-style marriage I instigated.'

'I only found out about the baby today.' The words seemed wrenched from her. 'It must have happened that first time...'

'Not a slow-gestating flu after all, huh? It's exciting, Claire. I like the idea of having a child with you. Will you give this a try?' He searched those deep brown eyes for a sign that she returned his feelings, even just a little. 'Will you let me love you, and try to love me in return?'

'*I can't.*' Claire's lips trembled. She closed her eyes and turned her face away. 'Oh, Lord. I can't do this.'

Her words struck deep. He hadn't expected them. He admitted that.

She didn't love him, and she didn't believe she ever could. He forced himself to his feet and left the room. Where did that leave them now?

CHAPTER THIRTEEN

NICHOLAS had arranged security for outside her hospital room door. Even after the way he had left her he'd been thinking of her.

Claire was deeply ashamed. When he had told her he loved her last night, guilt and remorse had choked her so much she hadn't even been able to respond. Oh, Lord, the joy of knowing that he loved her. And the agony of knowing she had ruined everything.

She took a deep breath, stepped from the taxi, and began to make her way up the path towards the house. Nicholas wouldn't be expecting her, she knew, but her night in the hospital had been so restless she had signed herself out at first light. She'd told the security guard her husband had sent a taxi for her. And now she was determined to do what she could to put this situation to rights.

Nicholas deserved to hear the truth, even though he would hate her when she told him.

I'll explain in a calm and concise manner. I won't be emotional, I'll simply stick to the facts and get it over with as fast as I can.

Damn, but her head ached.

Her inner dress rehearsal came to an abrupt halt when the front door flew open. Nicholas stood framed in the doorway. He was angry. She hadn't expected that. At least not yet.

'I'm sorry. I know I need to explain—' To her chagrin, a sob rose in her throat, choking off any chance of further words.

With a moan, she turned aside. Perhaps the taxi would still be there and she could get in it and just go away.

'Not so fast.' Nicholas's arms around her were surprisingly and oh-so-*achingly* gentle.

All the stresses of the past days and months seemed to coalesce into one big blazing lump deep down inside her. She wanted to bury her face against that solid, comforting chest and cry her heart out. But that wouldn't fix anything.

'Come inside, Claire.' He took her arm and hustled her inside the house, closing the door firmly behind them. 'I think we could do with some privacy.'

'Of course. I apologise.'

'Upstairs.' He gave the single word an edge of unmistakable command. 'We'll talk in the sitting room.'

'If you like.' It seemed ominous that she wasn't even to be offered a cup of tea or coffee, but she chastised herself. This was no social call. It would turn out to be the end of a marriage that should never have begun.

Once in the sitting room, Nicholas indicated the sofa. 'Make yourself comfortable there.' The anger was back again. 'You look as though you're about to fall down.'

She forced herself to sit right back in the enveloping comfort, and indeed did appreciate a chance to get off legs that had become less than supportive, to lay her aching head against the backrest.

'You signed yourself out of the hospital without allowing the doctor to check you over first.'

She shouldn't have been surprised. 'How did you know?'

'Security contacted me as soon as you left the building. They also followed your taxi here. You didn't think I'd take any chances, did you, after what happened yesterday?'

She might have known it wouldn't be that easy. 'The nursing staff watched me all night and everything was fine.' When that didn't seem to appease him, she lifted her hands in a gesture of supplication. 'I had to talk to you, Nicholas. I owe you that much.'

'In return for a declaration of love you didn't want to hear?' The words were spoken on a bitter shake of his head. 'Don't worry. I won't force you into a position where you have to pretend you have any feelings for me. You made it plain enough yesterday that you don't.'

Oh, no. She hadn't thought how he might have interpreted her silence. She couldn't bear for him to believe that. 'It's not that. I—'

'We'll go on as before.' His jaw was a wall of granite. 'I won't ask anything of you that you feel unable to give, but I will expect fidelity. I want your utter commitment to me and to our child. For his or her sake, we can at least pretend to be close.'

He squared his shoulders and breathed deeply.

'I won't tolerate separate lives, in the bedroom or in any other sense, but I don't blame you for this. I was the one who wanted a cold, calculated marriage. I was a fool.'

'I'm the one at fault, Nicholas.' She sat forward, her aching head forgotten in the urgency of stopping the flow of his words. She had to acknowledge her own guilt and wrongdoing. The scent of Nicholas's cologne teased her senses, so familiar, so treasured. She fought not to cry. 'It's been all my fault, right from the beginning.'

'You're not to blame for being unable to love me.' His lips twisted, and turbulence stirred again in the hazel eyes.

This was too much for Claire, and she shot to her feet. 'But I *do* love you,' she burst out, unable to hold back any longer. Her heart wouldn't let her. Not when Nicholas needed to hear this so much. It wouldn't be enough, in the end, but it was everything she had to give him and she would yield it gladly. 'That's the whole problem. I've loved you from the very start.'

At exactly the time she began to feel faint and realised she shouldn't have risen so quickly Nicholas reached for her.

But it would be disaster to let him hold her now. She could only take so much, and right now she was at her limits.

She threw up her hands. 'No. Don't touch me. I have to finish this. You have to hear it all. And then I'll leave, I promise you.'

'Whatever it is you have to say, Claire, I won't want you to leave. Not now that you've told me you love me.' He shook his head in emphasis but stepped back, allowing her to reclaim her seat without his help.

'I doubt you'll feel that way when I'm finished.' Her words strangled her, but she forced herself to go on. 'When I first got the opportunity to fill in as your personal assistant, it was like an answer to a prayer. I needed the extra money quite desperately. I didn't expect to fall in love.'

His eyebrows went up. She chose to believe it was because of the latter part of her statement, and gave a rueful smile. All the anxiety and pain, and he hadn't even guessed.

'You may look at me as though you don't believe it, but I fell for you very quickly. When you asked me to marry you I was already halfway there. It didn't take long for me to fall the rest of the way, although I fought it.'

'I *do* love you, too, Claire. I promise.'

Her heart tripped, but she shook her head. Oh, foolish hope. She couldn't entertain it any longer. 'You say that now, but you don't know what I've done to you.'

'What is this dreadful thing?' He crossed one foot over the other, drawing her attention to the muscled legs beneath the denim jeans. 'Not that measly little loan, I hope? I know about that. I assumed you must have had some debts. I'll pay it off and close it.'

Claire groaned. 'I think I'd better start from the beginning. I agreed to marry you when I never had any intention of following through on the plan.' When he went to speak, she held up a hand. 'Please. Let me finish it all before I lose my nerve.'

He inclined his head once. 'All right.'

'I pretended to be willing to marry you to buy more time in the position as your assistant.'

'In other words, you lied to me?'

She deserved the accusation, but coming from his lips it brought immeasurable pain. 'Yes. I lied. I let you believe I wanted the marriage when what I really wanted was time to save enough money for my needs.'

'What did you plan to do once you'd got this money? Why not simply help yourself to some of my funds once we were married? You must have known I would give it to you.'

'I was trying to be honourable.' How stupid that sounded now. How utterly ridiculous in the face of the way she had treated him. Inside, her heart begged him to at least *try* to understand a little. 'You see, I couldn't afford to lose the job, and you threatened to send me back to the clerical pool if I didn't agree to marry you.'

'I did not—' He cut himself off, paused, and rubbed his forehead with the tips of two fingers. 'I suppose that's true. But why did you need the money so much? What was it for?'

'It was to protect Sophie. She'd stolen from her boss, and he found her out and blackmailed her over it. Either she paid back all she owed him, plus bags more, or he'd get her sent to jail for embezzling. It would have killed her, and ruined Tom's career as well.'

'So Sophie ran to you.' His hands clenched. 'Haven't you ever wanted to take that sister of yours and wrap your hands around her silly neck?'

'Quite frequently.' It was the first time Claire had smiled since she arrived, even if the smile was twisted with a string of unhappy memories. 'But I love Sophie. I couldn't bear the thought that she might end up in jail for embezzlement, and she is trying to do better now, Nicholas. Really.'

All of a sudden his gaze narrowed. 'That was the reason for the loan—to pay this blackmailer? Was it the same man who attacked you in the parking lot at Monroe's?'

'Yes. I made what I believed was the final payment to him, but then he said I had to pay another seven hundred and fifty thousand.'

She shuddered, remembering the crazed glint in Haynes's eyes that day. She had put Nicholas's life in danger, and then hers and the baby's. How could she have thought she'd have any protection against someone like that? She should have recognised the danger then, and told Nicholas the truth and faced the consequences. Not let it get to the point that it had.

'He gave me three days to get the first ten per cent. I couldn't.' The anxiety of that time still had the power to make her tremble. 'I paid a homeless man to deliver a message to Haynes, saying I needed a month and that I'd have to pay in smaller instalments. I thought I could get him to agree to that. I was wrong.'

Nicholas's face was carved in granite, his eyes hard, but Claire forced herself to go on.

'He threatened to hurt you if I didn't pay him. I couldn't go to the police. It would have exposed Sophie, and you would have realised I'd been deceiving you and thrown me out, where I couldn't watch out for you. All I could do was make sure I was there to protect you myself.'

'You could have told me.' He leapt from his chair, his hands clenched. 'My God, Claire. *I* would have protected *you*.'

'Even after I'd lied from the start?' She shook her head. 'You'd have ended the marriage, and then there would have been nobody to take care of you. I watched you all the time, worrying, and hoped that when I met with Haynes he would agree to my terms. I paid him ten thousand dollars and tried to reason with him, but he was incensed. He made more threats. Told me I had to come up with sixty-five thousand.' Her voice started to wobble, and she stopped to take a breath. 'There were only a few more days to go before I had to pay it. I was desperate. I didn't know what I was going to do. Then I realised I'd missed a period and found out I was pregnant. So much has happened. I can't believe that was only yesterday. Before I had a chance to even take the news in Haynes tried to kidnap me. He'd decided to make you pay ransom instead of trying to get money out of me.'

'I'll kill him myself.' Nicholas ground the words out.

She bit her lip.

Nicholas's eyes narrowed. 'There's more, isn't there?'

'He said he was going to kill me afterwards.'

'He'll go to jail for that.' Anger still radiated from Nicholas, but he sat back down again. 'I have power, Claire. He can tell the police anything he likes, but I'll make sure Sophie's story never gets out. Haynes will pay for what he has done to us. We won't be paying for anything else.' He drew a shuddering breath. 'When I think what could have happened to you. Damn it, Claire, I love you. I don't ever want to see you at risk again.'

'You can't still love me. I've married you under false pretences.' Her hands plucked at the fabric of her skirt, leaving little creases in the material. 'I owe you for the money we spent on the wedding ceremony. And you bought me a car that will have to be sold off. And I took out that bank loan on your good name. I'll try to pay it all back somehow. I put your life at risk, and the baby's.'

Tears threatened again, and she blinked them back furiously. Later she could break down and cry until there was nothing left, but not yet. Not now.

'If I had stuck to my convictions and at least not slept with you I wouldn't be pregnant, but I can't be sorry for it. I want your baby. At least I'll have something of you. And I promise I won't trouble you ever again if I can just keep that much and the memories of those times in your arms.'

'You really haven't been listening, have you?' Nicholas's words were fierce, but his gaze was gentle. He stood and pulled Claire upwards and forward, until their bodies melded and his hands closed around her upper arms. 'You said you love me. Was that the truth, or were you trying to soften the blow of everything else?'

'It was true.' She made the confession to his shirt-front, unwilling to see the pity in his eyes if she met him stare for stare. 'It *is* true. I love you, and I've had the chance to be married to you, and I'm thankful for that much.'

'And you're just going to give up and walk away from anything else you might be able to have?' He shook her slightly until she did look up, and their gazes clashed.

'This isn't some security system problem, to be worked through to a suitable solution.' She tried to break free of his hold but he tightened his grip. 'I can't fix this, Nicholas. I've messed up, big-time, and there's not a thing I can do about it now except to say that I'm sorry and ask for your forgiveness—if you can ever manage to give it.'

He gave her shoulders another slight shake. 'I don't know what I want to do the most. Take you to our room and love you senseless, or turn you over my knee and paddle that lovely backside until you see reason.'

'Wh—what do you mean?' Her heart thundered as she stared at him. 'Why would you want to make love after all that I've confessed?'

'I keep saying it, Claire. I love you. I want a beginning today, not an ending. If there's anything to forgive, consider it forgiven.'

Oh, those words were sweet. Was it possible? Could he truly love her after all that had happened?

'I've done so much to wrong you.'

'I wronged you, too, by asking you to marry me without love.' His hands clenched and unclenched as he faced her. 'Will you be married to me for real? Will you live with me and be in love with me, as I'm in love with you?'

'Nicholas, yes. If you really mean it.' She breathed the words through a mist of hope and love. 'There's nothing in the world that I want more than to be with you for the rest of my life.'

'Then come closer.' His voice was hoarse and oddly roughened, his eyes bright with emotion. 'I want to hold my wife and my child in my arms.'

'And I—*we* want to be held.' She flew into his arms. 'I don't deserve you. I don't deserve *this*. But I'm going to take it anyway. I love you too much to walk away unless you tell me I have to.'

'That will never happen. And I don't want to hear you speak of being undeserving ever again. We've both used each other, in different ways. Now the past is behind us—forgotten. From now on we focus on the present, and the future.' His lips came down on hers in heated, demanding splendour.

Claire met his hunger with matching need, and surrendered willingly in a mist of love for this man who had stolen her heart.

When he raised his head his gaze searched hers with utter tenderness, and her heart melted for him all over again. She raised a shaky hand to cup his face, simply enjoying the feel of him, the texture and shape of him.

He turned his face into her hand and kissed the palm. 'I want to make love with you.'

'Then let's go to bed.'

She took his hand and tugged him towards the bedroom. Their bedroom, she realised, for the rest of their lives together. The thought brought a fresh wave of emotion, and with it came a matching need to love him in that most intimate of ways.

At the door of the room, Nicholas stopped her. 'This is selfish of me. You're just out of hospital—and there's the baby to think of.'

'The baby is safely cocooned, and will be thoroughly impervious to what its parents are about.' She clasped his hands in hers and brought them, joined, to rest against her heart. 'As for the rest, I may not feel a hundred per cent, but I know you'll be gentle with me. And I'm fairly certain that I'll expire if you *don't* make me yours again right now.'

He lowered her to the bed and removed her garments one by one until she lay naked and waiting before him. His gaze moved over her slowly. 'I've never seen anything as wonderfully made, as perfect.'

His words heated her as nothing else could have. She reached out her arms. 'Then come here to me. Let me hold you and feel for myself that I don't ever have to let you go.'

He shed his clothes and stretched out beside her, and proceeded to adore her body until she couldn't remember where she ended and he began. When they rose to the heights and fell together she called his name and cried in his arms. He cried with her, the barriers finally down.

Claire fell asleep. When she woke, Nicholas was sitting on the edge of the bed, watching her.

'Let's go out onto the balcony.'

He made tea, and they sat beside the enclosed area of the Jacuzzi, sipping the hot, fragrant blend.

Suddenly Nicholas spoke. 'While you were sleeping, I got a phone call.'

Her hand jerked. She put the cup down carefully and turned to him. 'Was it Haynes? Was he making more threats?'

'No, it wasn't Haynes. But it was about him.' He put his tea down, too, and looked at her solemnly. 'The police caught him just this side of the Queensland border. It seems he'd realised he was in trouble and was trying to get away.'

'So he's in custody?'

'Yes.' Nicholas took one of her hands and held it inside his. 'It turns out you aren't the only one he's been blackmailing. There's so much evidence against him he'll be going to jail for a very long time.'

'Oh, thank God.' Claire wasn't sure how, but she found herself on her feet and held in Nicholas's secure embrace. She pressed her face to his chest, comforted by the steady beat of his heart. 'I want to feel sorry for him, but I'm so relieved he's been put away. I don't think I ever really realised how truly evil he was.'

Nicholas stroked her hair and pressed a kiss to the top of her head, then pulled back to look into her eyes. 'Tom and Sophie will have to be told, but I'll leave that to you. I realise Sophie still has to confess to her husband. For now, I want you and I to focus on *us*. We have a lot of ground to make up for in this marriage of ours.'

'We do, don't we?' She smiled. 'I feel as though our marriage is truly just beginning.' She reached up and drew his head to hers. 'I love you, Nicholas Monroe, with all my heart. I'm thrilled to be your wife, and to be having your baby.'

He kissed her hard, then drew back. 'There is one thing we've yet to do, that I've dreamed of since I first brought you here.'

'What is it?' At that moment she would have flown to the moon had he asked her. 'I'll do anything you like. Anything that makes you happy.'

'Will you?' He pretended to consider this offer, but his eyes twinkled and he quickly let her off the hook, glancing at the Jacuzzi behind them. 'I hinted at it once before, when we talked about you becoming my willing slave. It's quite simple, Claire. I want to initiate you into the pleasures of bathing together on the balcony.'

She pouted, entering into the game. 'Just bathing? Is that the best you can offer?'

He took her hand and led her towards the secluded enclosure. 'Oh, I think I may be able to make it a little more interesting than that for my lovely wife.'

'I should think so, too.' She spoiled the haughty comment by bursting into a sunny smile and throwing her arms around him again. 'I love you, Nicholas.'

'I love you too, my lovely lady.' He drew her towards him with a purposeful look in his eye. 'Let me show you just how much.'

EPILOGUE

THE floral borders looked their best at this time of year. Claire's gaze passed over them, then roamed through the smattering of family and guests in the spacious backyard until it came to rest on her husband, where he stood talking to Tom Cranshaw.

Nicholas held his baby daughter in the crook of his arm. Jemima was wriggling and cooing, enjoying the warm day as her daddy played with her bare toes beneath the Christening gown. The outfit had started out with matching silken booties, but their daughter had worked her way free of them as usual.

Claire's heart swelled with love as she studied the two most precious people in her life. After the initial sickness, her pregnancy had been uncomplicated. Nicholas had spoiled her, and after Jemima had arrived had spread the net to include spoiling his daughter as well.

279

It must run in the family. Damon and Colin, Nicholas's brothers, were both madly in love with Jemima already. Damon was planning her stock portfolio, and Colin never missed a chance to hold her.

They were all here today. Nicholas's brothers, and his parents—although the latter were at separate ends of the yard, of course. But they had both taken surprisingly well to grandparenthood.

Dianna—she couldn't live with being called Nana or Gran—had shown Claire a beautiful massage technique to use on Jemima just after she was born. Nicholas's mother was often self-interested, but she had given that much.

And Granpa Monroe—no such qualms in his case—had built Jemima the most gorgeous hand-crafted nursery set. Cradle, cot and rocking horse.

Family. Claire looked back at her husband, then let her gaze rove to his companion. Tom had a baby in his grasp, too. Eliza Claire Cranshaw was older and more sturdy than Jemima, but seemed to have just as much determination in her genes. At present she was attempting to chew the end off her proud father's spotted red and black tie.

Tom didn't even notice. Nor had he seemed to care when Eliza had offered the same service to one or two of the political dignitaries he'd invited along today.

'I know this party is for our daughters, but I have something for you, too, Claire.'

Sophie had approached without Claire realising. Now she held out a gift bag with a pretty gold tag attached.

The guests had showered the baby cousins with gifts after the Christening service at the chapel where Nicholas and Claire had married. Sophie had pitched in to help organise this party, but that was supposed to be all. She wasn't supposed to be giving Claire a gift.

Claire eyed the glossy bag warily, and suddenly Sophie laughed.

'Go on.' She pushed the bag into Claire's hands. 'Look inside.'

Claire did, and then she laughed too, and her eyes filled with tears. She pulled out the figurine and smiled. It was an excellent likeness of a mopoke, and across its delicately coloured middle were the words *'Wise Old Owl'*.

Sophie hugged her quickly, then stepped back. 'You are, you know. If not for all you've done for me I wouldn't be here with Tom today, with no secrets between us, happy with our daughter and our lives.'

Claire sniffed and wiped her eyes with the back of her free hand. 'Thank you.' She glanced down at the owl. 'It's a lovely sentiment—although I'm not so sure about the "old" part.'

Sophie smiled. As she did, Claire saw Tom look over at her and his face soften. Claire's gaze went to Nicholas again. He sent her a look of such love and promise that she choked up all over again before she turned back to her sister.

'I hope you saved up for this, Sophie.' She tried to sound stern. 'It must have cost you at least ten dollars.' She pictured Sophie pulling it from a shelf at a chainstore. 'Maybe even twenty.'

Sophie turned the figurine over in Claire's hands to show her the discreet imprint on the bottom. 'Closer to five hundred, actually. But who's counting?'

Claire gasped.

'Don't worry.' Sophie gave her a grin that was pure mischief. 'I may never lose my taste for the expensive, but I *am* reformed. I budgeted for this item, and when I told my husband about it he was so proud of me he gave me a raise in my allowance.'

'Oh, Sophie.' Claire gave way to helpless giggles, then she sobered and looked her sister full in the eyes. 'I love you. I hope you know that.'

'I do. And I love you, too.' Sophie sniffed, then took Claire's arm with a determined air. 'And now I think it's time we rescued those husbands of ours. Who knows? Maybe we'll make it over there before our daughters wind them completely around their baby-soft fingers.'

Claire glanced again at the tableau under the trees. She shook her head and let the happiness swell inside her. 'I think it's already too late.'

MILLS & BOON® PUBLISH EIGHT LARGE PRINT TITLES A MONTH. THESE ARE THE EIGHT TITLES FOR SEPTEMBER 2005

THE ITALIAN'S STOLEN BRIDE
Emma Darcy

THE PURCHASED WIFE
Michelle Reid

BOUND BY BLACKMAIL
Kate Walker

PUBLIC WIFE, PRIVATE MISTRESS
Sarah Morgan

THEIR PREGNANCY BOMBSHELL
Barbara McMahon

THE CORPORATE MARRIAGE CAMPAIGN
Leigh Michaels

A MOTHER FOR HIS DAUGHTER
Ally Blake

THE BOSS'S CONVENIENT BRIDE
Jennie Adams

MILLS & BOON®

Live the emotion

0805 Rom

MILLS & BOON® PUBLISH EIGHT LARGE PRINT TITLES A MONTH. THESE ARE THE EIGHT TITLES FOR OCTOBER 2005

❦

MARRIED BY ARRANGEMENT
Lynne Graham

PREGNANCY OF REVENGE
Jacqueline Baird

IN THE MILLIONAIRE'S POSSESSION
Sara Craven

THE ONE-NIGHT WIFE
Sandra Marton

THE ITALIAN'S RIGHTFUL BRIDE
Lucy Gordon

HUSBAND BY REQUEST
Rebecca Winters

CONTRACT TO MARRY
Nicola Marsh

THE MIRRABROOK MARRIAGE
Barbara Hannay

MILLS & BOON®

Live the emotion

0905 Rom LP